THE SUMMER OF THE CROWS

Tony Ducklow

To Joanna,
Best wishes!

Tony
Ducklow

ISBN: 978-1-4611-1893-0

Snowman photograph by Teri Eckholm

To my old friends and neighbors

CONTENTS

1
SCHOOL'S OUT FOR SUMMER!

"FIVE...FOUR...THREE...TWO...ONE!" SHOUTED THE voices from room 1334. The bell sounded and a deafening cheer rang through the fifth grade classroom at L.C. Webster Elementary School. It was a Friday on the last day of school. Students were giving one another high fives. Girls were hugging and crying. Boys were slapping each other on the back. In a few minutes most of the students had filed out of the room. All but Tucker McTeal.

Tucker turned, looked over his shoulder and waved a last goodbye to his teacher, Mrs. Field. He liked her because she was unusual and unpredictable and she couldn't pass up having some fun while she taught. At the end of a social studies lesson she once said, in all seriousness, "So in closing, always remember that those that forget the pasta are doomed to reheat it." The students stared back blankly at her.

"Uh, Mrs. Field, what exactly does that mean? What does microwaving cold pasta have to do with Germany and World War II?" someone finally asked.

"Absolutely nothing!" she proudly proclaimed.

"Well then why did you..."

"On the other hand, I might be able to make a case for Italy. Italians are known for their spaghetti," she interrupted, "and that makes me hungry. Put your books in your desk and let's go to lunch." Weeks later while Tucker was playing a video game that was set in World War II called *Hitler Must Be Destroyed!,* he heard a general proclaim, "Those who forget the past are doomed to repeat it!" He paused the game and thought about it for a moment. Then he smiled and said, "Those that forget the pasta are doomed to reheat it." *She sure does have a strange sense of humor*, he thought.

The year had gone by quickly, even for Tucker, who hated being cooped up in school all day. He looked over the classroom one last time. He smiled, nodded at Mrs. Field and started walking toward the door. Then he heard her voice shout, "Hey Kiddo, not so fast, I have a twenty-five year old dead rabbit for you!"

"Yes!" he said, giving a fist pump.

He knew exactly what she meant. The dead rabbit in question was actually a still-born baby bunny in a glass container about the size of a jelly jar. It was preserved in some kind of clear liquid. Mrs. Field was given the jar over two decades ago by a roommate who created the unusual item while she was enrolled in a college biology class. It was on display in Mrs. Field's classroom along with a mounted billy goat head (named Fred), various rock collections, assorted snake skins that had been shed, a steer skull, terrariums that held everything from skinks to box turtles and aquariums that had everything from whiptail catfish to bucktooth tetra. There was also Mr. Phinneas T.

Pettibone, the full-sized human skeleton that hung in the corner of the classroom. Mrs. Field claimed he was made of plastic, but he looked pretty real to Tucker.

She walked over and handed the jar to him. The baby bunny, with its eyes closed, appeared peaceful and serene as it floated weightlessly in its little glass world. On days that Tucker arrived a bit early to class, it was one of his favorite things to look at in the room. Even though the rabbit was born many years ago, the liquid had preserved it so perfectly that it appeared as if it was born just yesterday. He held the jar close to his face and stared at it. There were times during the year that he had stared at it so long and hard that he had almost convinced himself that he had seen the rabbit move.

"Have a good break, Kiddo. And it wouldn't kill you to work on your math skills this summer. Ride your bike by my house sometime and I'll give you some packets that'll help you sharpen your skills."

"As if!" Tucker thought, but said, "Yeah, okay, maybe I will. Hey, thanks for the rabbit. It's pretty cool."

He studied it again for a moment before putting it in his backpack. While he was appreciative of the gift, the talk about math and doing packets during the summer made his skin crawl and he knew it was time to leave.

"See you, Mrs. Field!" he shouted and dashed out through the classroom door.

"Hey, Poodles, wait up!" "Poodles" was short for Poodlehead, Poodleboy, and Poodlesheep. While he didn't mind the various Poodle nicknames, Scotty Nova was not fond of Poodlesheep. His name changed the day his family brought home a curly-haired white poodle a few years back. He was pretty proud of his new puppy and he took it around the neighborhood, showing it off to all his friends. As he came across a group of his friends playing kickball in the court, or as adults called it, the "cul-de-sac," one of the kids (a boy named Crandal Bino-Grimes, to be specific) noticed that Scotty's blonde, almost white curly hair was nearly identical to the dog's fur. The next day Crandal joked that after seeing Scotty's dog, he thought Scotty himself had a poodle head. From that day on Scotty was called Poodlehead.

Poodlehead was already halfway across the softball field on the school grounds and making his way home; he wasted no time getting out of the school building after the bell rang. The boys lived just blocks from each other and walked the mile to school together every day. Poodlehead had been one of his best friends for almost as long as Tucker could remember.

Poodlehead turned toward Tucker and sang, "School's out for summer! School's out forever!" They both laughed. Despite backpacks loaded with everything that could be crammed into them on the last day of school, they both felt like they were walking on air.

"What's the first thing you're gonna do?" asked Poodlehead.

"What do you think?"

"*Revenge of the Rabid Leprechauns*!" they both shouted as they leaped high into the air and gave each other high fives.

"I can't believe the moment has finally arrived!" said Tucker.

Rabid Leprechauns was their favorite video game series of all time. They'd already played and conquered *Rabid Leprechauns, Planet of the Rabid Leprechauns, The Wrath of the Rabid Leprechauns* and *Rabid Leprechauns: McCrud Strikes Back. Revenge of the Rabid Leprechauns* had just gone on sale the day before and they had yet to play it. Tucker's mother had promised to pick up the new game for him when she went out shopping.

"You'll never get me four-leaf clover of death or me pot o' radioactive gold!" Poodlehead exclaimed in a fairly decent Irish accent, and attempted to do a jig. He picked up a stick from the ground and shook it at Tucker.

"I'll knock your head off with me shillelagh!" Aside from being rabid, some of the more powerful leprechauns could obtain a shillelagh (shi-lay-lee), a heavy wooden walking cane that could also be used as a club for fighting or even for swordplay.

"And then I'll eat your brains before you get close to any of me treasures!" Poodlehead made sloppy chewing noises and let some drool seep out the side of his mouth in an attempt to look like a foamy-mouthed leprechaun.

"That's because me brains are magically delicious!" Tucker responded in his own Irish accent.

"Wouldn't it be great if we were really rabid leprechauns? No one would ever, ever mess with us! We could even boss adults around. They'd be too afraid to disobey us!"

"You're crazy, Poodles!" Tucker shouted with a laugh. He had never told anyone, but he'd actually had dreams where he was in fact a rabid leprechaun.

"I can't wait! What time should I come for the sleepover tonight?" Poodlehead asked.

"I think about seven. That's what I told the other guys." Meaning Benny Xiong, Josh Deeds and Crandal Bino-Grimes. Their end-of-the-year sleepover was now a four-year tradition.

"Okay, okay, okay," Poodlehead said excitedly, "you just have to promise me not to open *Revenge of the Rabid Leprechauns* until I get there. Don't even take it out of the wrapper! Wait; don't even take it out of the bag! Wait, wait, wait, don't EVEN look at the bag! You gotta promise!" Poodlehead pleaded.

"What's the difference if I look at the bag?"

"Because if you look at the bag, you'll take it out of the bag. If you take it out of the bag, you'll take it out if its wrapper. If you take it out of the wrapper, you'll open up the game. If you open up the game, you'll want to play it. It's like that *If You Give a Moose a Cookie* book. I just have to be there with you when the new game first comes on the screen!"

"Mouse."

"What?"

"It's *If You Give a **Mouse** a Cookie*. The other book is "*If You Give a Moose a Muffin*."

"Whatever!" Poodlehead answered in exasperation. "I just gotta be there. You gotta promise!"

"Are you saying that I can't even take it out of the bag to look at the cover?"

"No! I mean yes! You know what will happen!"

"All right, all right. I promise."

"Excell-aun-tay, grome-ay-graun-tay!" exclaimed Poodlehead. The phrase was something they'd both been using for a long time. Neither of them knew where it came from, but they liked saying it.

The boys continued their walk home, energized by their thoughts of what might transpire that evening. The early summer sun felt good on their backs after a brutally cold winter. A Minnesota winter doesn't like to let go easily and sometimes will even stretch its cold fingers deep into April. They talked about the rumors they'd heard about the latest version of *Rabid Leprechauns* and the strategies that they planned on using to defeat the game.

"I'm pretty sure that the Ninja Munchkins will be back," Tucker said.

"No way, no how. We both know that the Ninja Munchkins were the eternal arch-enemies of the Rabid Leprechauns but they were finally all killed off in *The Wrath of the Rabid Leprechauns*. Remember, they were wiped out when the Leprechauns had no choice but to join forces with the Insane Robot Assassins and the Zombie Carp?"

"Duh! Who doesn't? But Crandal told me that the last *Rabid Leprechauns* game didn't sell as well as the past games so they decided to bring back the Ninja Munchkins."

"Huh." Poodles appeared stunned. He stopped walking for a moment to think things over.

"That would be impossible," he muttered. "That would be totally impossible! How could they come back from being extinct? Nothing can come back from being extinct." His face was intense from the thought and his eyebrows were wrinkled. "They were all totally vaporized when their planet exploded! That means no DNA. DNA is the only thing that can bring you back when you're extinct. You know, the way they bring back dinosaurs in the movies."

Both boys were silent and thought about it for a moment.

Finally, Tucker had an idea. "What if there was one Ninja Munchkin left? One hiding on a spaceship that blasted off right before the planet was vaporized?"

"Nope. I clearly remember hearing the narrator of the game proclaim there wasn't a Ninja Munchkin left alive in the Leprechaunical Galaxy. If they bring back the Ninja Munchkins, the game won't seem real anymore. I mean, how can they think anyone would believe something like that?"

Tucker agreed. That was totally ridiculous and unbelievable.

2
MAD DOG AND BLACK HOLES

THE BOYS MADE their way up the hill to their neighborhood and parted a block from Tucker's house. Tucker ran the remaining block home. He was glad to be done with school and, in his mind, crossing into his yard officially started the first day of summer vacation. He ran up the hill that was in the front of his house and then around to the back door where he entered and tossed his backpack on the floor.

"Pick up your backpack, and hang it in the corner," said a small voice from the kitchen.

"Mind your own business, Mad Dog."

"Fine, don't do it then. I'll just tell."

"Rrrrrghhhhhh!" Tucker growled under his breath as he walked back and picked up his backpack and hung it on a peg on the wall. "I'll just tell, I'll just tell…" he muttered in a whiney voice.

"Are you happy now, Maddy?" he barked.

"You should just do stuff like that yourself without anyone telling you to do it. The house would stay a lot cleaner that way." Maddy brushed her long dark brown hair away from her big brown eyes and continued coloring a picture of a unicorn at the kitchen table.

Madeline, or Maddy as most people called her, was the oldest of Tucker's three younger sisters; they were all born one year apart. All of them still had to take the bus home from school. This meant Maddy got home before Tucker and always seemed to be right there waiting for him when he walked through the kitchen door. While she may have been a couple of years younger, she could hold her own whenever they got into an argument, which frustrated Tucker.

Seeing Maddy waiting for him at the kitchen table every day was like a pebble in Tucker's shoe. He really disliked being nagged or told what to do by a younger sibling. But then again, just about everything Maddy said or did seemed to rub him the wrong way. She was always asking him questions, threatening to tell on him, or pestering him about one thing or another. She also had the knack for being a distraction and interrupting him when was doing his favorite thing in life—playing video games.

How could he ever forget the time that he was only moments away from conquering The Phlegm Beast from the Cesspool of Death when she not only walked right in front of the screen, but then bumped right into the game system? The bump had caused the system to freeze up, which meant he had to reboot the game and start all over again. Who could blame him for losing his temper and yelling at her? She began crying and had the nerve to run and go tell on *him!* It was totally unfair that his parents ended up punishing him instead of her.

"Are your friends coming over tonight?" Maddy inquired.

"What do you think?" he asked, annoyed. "You know we have a sleepover every year after the last day of school."

"Do you want me to help? I could make some flavored drink mix for you. I'm pretty good at making it now you know, especially cherry flavor."

"Me and my friends don't drink baby drinks anymore. We all drink *KaBlam! Cola* now. '*KaBlam! Cola*, As much caffeine as the law allows!'" Tucker said, imitating the announcer's voice from the commercials. He suddenly wondered if people would get arrested if they put just one drop more of caffeine in the drink.

"How about popcorn? I could make microwave popcorn for you guys."

"Maddy, the only reason you want to do these things is so that you can come down the basement and bug us. And you know that ain't happenin'!"

"Aw, come on! Just for a little while? I promise I will just sit quietly and watch. I won't bother anyone."

"As if!" Tucker answered. "As if!" was one of his favorite phrases of all time. "You know you wouldn't last five minutes before you'd be begging us to play the games too. That's what you always do."

"I promise I won't do it this time. I really, really promise!"

"Give it up, Mad Dog. You're not coming down the basement and bugging us while we play *Rabid Leprechauns*. It just came out today and it's been untouched by human hands. Or even contaminated nonhuman hands like yours. I don't want you spoiling anything."

For once Maddy didn't say a thing. She just sat there and smiled. This was quite unusual for her and made Tucker very suspicious.

"What are you smiling at?"

"Nothing," she answered with the grin still on her face. .

She finally blurted out, "I already played your stupid game."

"As if."

"As if to you!" Maddy shot back. "I had a doctor's appointment this afternoon and Mom had to pick me up early from school. She let me play *Rabid Leprechauns* when we got home."

"No way! You're lying," Tucker said with a chuckle. But there was some doubt in his voice, and for one brief moment, a hint of fear entered Tucker's eyes.

That moment was all Maddy needed and her face lit up in satisfaction.

"I got attacked by this weird creature called a Karate Clown! I kept trying to bite him on his humongous clown feet with my leprechaun. Man, those clowns can do awesome karate kicks!" she said with a giggle.

"Yeah, right. I'm not buying it Mad Dog." He grabbed a glass from the cupboard and filled it with water, trying hard to appear bored by the conversation.

"He kicked me so hard I went into a black hole. I think I went back in time or something."

"I'm so sure," he said, rolling his eyes, and he began to drink from his cup. He was still attempting to act like he wasn't the least bit bothered by her comments. But then he played back the words "black hole" and "back in time" in his head and suddenly a chill went down his spine.

"I couldn't believe there were Ninja Munchkins in there! I thought you told me they were gone for good."

Tucker choked on the water and it sprayed out of his mouth. Luckily, he was standing in front of the sink.

"Mom!" Tucker bellowed between his coughing fit. Time travel, of course! That's how the Ninja Munchkins returned! He was enraged. He couldn't believe it. How could his mother betray him like that? He ran over to the kitchen table, grabbed Maddy's picture of the unicorn and crumpled it up. The smug smile vanished from her face and tears filled her eyes. She tilted back her head, opened her mouth so wide you could see the three fillings in her back teeth and screeched, "Mom!" They both scrambled out of the kitchen in search of their mother.

Megan McTeal was in the back bedroom helping Emily and Olivia sort out all the items they had brought home in their backpacks.

The screams and sounds of Tucker's and Maddy's stomping feet echoed through the McTeal house as the two dashed toward the back bedroom. Tucker burst through the door first.

"I can't believe you let her play my *Rabid Leprechauns* game! I haven't even seen it yet and she's already played it and now she's ruined it for me! It's my game! My game!"

Maddy was right behind him, sobbing and screaming and crying as if she had lost a limb in a farm accident. She dramatically held out the crumpled unicorn picture in front of her mother's face. She tried to talk but could only get one word at a time out before she'd gasp for air.

"He…*gasp*…ruined…*gasp*…my…*gasp*…unicorn… picture…for…*gasp*…for…

for..for…NO…REASON…*gasp!*"

Mrs. McTeal sighed and pushed her long brown hair, which was almost identical to Maddy's, away from her face and sat on the edge of the bed. Emily and Olivia looked at each other and decided that this was their chance to escape having to sort out their backpacks with their mother. They quickly slipped out of the room while she was distracted and went out to play in the backyard.

"Oh honey, come here," she said to Maddy, holding her arms open. Then she looked at Tucker.

"Why? Why do you do things like this?" she asked, while displaying the crumpled paper.

"Because she…"

Tucker's mother held up her hand palm forward, showing she didn't really want to hear his answer.

"What have we told you about picking on someone younger than you? You're old enough now not to be bullying your sister like that. Yes, I did let her play the game. And let me remind you that it is not your game…"

"But I'm going to pay…" he interrupted. His mother put her hand up again to stop him.

"…yet. It is not your game yet. Yes, you have promised to work it off by doing jobs around the house. But as of now, you haven't paid a cent toward it."

Tucker quickly glanced over at Maddy. She was tucked up underneath her mother's right arm, snuggled up next to her. Why didn't his mother ever listen to his side of the story? Why didn't she ever notice how quickly Maddy was always able to stop crying when she was able to get her way? Tucker gritted his teeth. He could feel the anger bubbling up deep inside him. It seemed it always went down like this. No matter what the situation was with his younger siblings, especially Maddy, he could never win. Maddy's eyes met Tucker's and she flashed him a smug little smile on her tear-stained face.

"Arghhhhh!" he screamed as he stomped his feet and pointed at Maddy. "You see! You see! She did it again! She just smiled at me!"

Mrs. McTeal's face grew tight and she rose to her feet. "You are having your friends over tonight for the sleepover. If you can't behave any better than this, I'll talk to your dad about it when he gets home from work and we'll cancel the whole thing."

The bubbling anger melted quickly away and it was replaced by panic and a sinking feeling in his stomach. He and his friends had been talking about the sleepover for weeks and he'd never live it down if it got cancelled. He had to be careful now.

He took a deep breath.

"I'm okay now, Mom. You're right, it's not my game yet and I shouldn't have gotten so mad at Maddy. Maddy,

I'm sorry for crumpling your paper. I shouldn't have gotten so upset about you playing my...the game." But in his mind he said, "As if!" and hid his crossed fingers behind his back.

His mother smiled and stroked the side of his face.

"That's what I like to hear. Can you give your sister a hug?"

This was how it always seemed to end; him having to take the blame and then having to hug his sister. Maddy eagerly came forward and wrapped her arms around him and squeezed. He put his arms around her and played the part. But he didn't mean it. Not one little bit.

3
TUCKER'S SECRET

THE DOORBELL RANG and Tucker raced for the door. "I got it!" he yelled.

Bandit, the McTeal family dog, began yapping and jumping excitedly at the door. The white pug (at least that's what the family thought he mostly was) never met anyone he didn't like. Tucker looked out the window and saw Benny standing there. He was holding his sleeping bag under one arm and a backpack under the other. Tucker pulled open the door. Tucker's eyes met Benny's and they grinned.

"C'mon in, Benny!" Tucker said excitedly, motioning him in. He was a stocky boy with thick black hair, a ready smile, and just a hint of mischievousness on his round face. His father was right behind him and followed Benny into the house.

"Hey, Bandit, how you doing?" Benny shouted as he bent over to play with the dog. Benny loved animals, any kind of animal really, but he especially loved dogs. Bandit's large pug eyes looked up at Benny with love and appreciation as Benny stroked the top of his head and scratched him under his chin.

"I sure wish I had a dog," he said.

Mr. Xiong, who was Hmong, looked coldly at the dog. "Dog a lot of work. When he get sick, too much money to pay."

Mr. Xiong was older than many of the other dads in the neighborhood. In fact, Benny had a brother that was even older than Tucker's father. Mr. Xiong rarely smiled and seemed to take life very seriously. He was not a very tall man, but he was powerfully built. Benny had told Tucker that his dad had been a soldier in a country called Laos. Benny would sometimes beg his father to tell him war stories, but his dad never talked about it much. "That long time ago and I don't remember anymore," was all he would say. Mr. Xiong spoke English, but it was sometimes hard for him. Tucker's dad said he thought Mr. Xiong had probably seen some terrible things over in Laos and Vietnam and that it might be the reason why he was so serious most of the time. Benny had told Tucker that to avoid being killed, his dad had escaped into Thailand. Tucker and Benny thought it all sounded pretty exciting, especially where Mr. Xiong had to swim across a river in the middle of the night. Both of Benny's parents had to live in something called a refugee camp for years after they had escaped into Thailand. Benny said that it had never become safe for his parents to go back to Laos and that's why they ended up living in the United States.

"Mr. Xiong, good to see you again! Benny, you look bigger and stronger every time I see you!" Ethan McTeal said as he entered the room and extended his hand to Mr. Xiong. Ethan was Tucker's father and he was at least six inches taller than Benny's dad. He was rather slim and had a smile on his face most of the time. Mr. Xiong nodded and gave a half-smile, shaking Mr. McTeal's hand.

"Thank you for letting Kong stay at your house." Benny was called Kong most of the time by his father. Many of the Hmong kids that Tucker knew had two names, a Hmong name and an American name.

"Be good boy, Kong," Mr. Xiong ordered.

"I will," Benny said with a smile. Tucker motioned toward the door with his head and they both dashed off toward the basement.

"Does Benny need to be home at any certain time tomorrow?" asked Mr. McTeal.

"Anytime you want him to go," replied Mr. Xiong.

Mr. McTeal laughed. "Well, we always enjoy Benny. I'm sure there won't be any reason for us to want him to go."

Mr. Xiong didn't laugh back or smile.

"Okay, thank you," Mr. Xiong said. He then turned and walked out the door.

"Who was that?" asked Mrs. McTeal as she came into the kitchen. She'd just finished helping Emily and Olivia with their evening baths and then into their pajamas. Maddy was in her room watching a video. "One of our overnight guests?"

"Yep, it was Benny and his dad."

"Did he look like this?" she asked, getting a very serious look on her face.

"Yeah, pretty much. But he wasn't quite as cute as you." He leaned forward and gave her a quick kiss.

"Ewwww! I saw that!" said Maddy as she entered the kitchen.

"Hey, Mom, can I help you make snacks for the boys?

"Hmmmm," she said. "I was thinking about that. Maybe they think they're too old for that stuff now."

"I think we should make them flavored drinks and popcorn. You know how good I am at making the cherry flavored kind!"

Mrs. McTeal thought about it for a moment.

"Can I help serve them, too?"

"Well if you're going to all the trouble to help make it, I think it's only fair that you get to help serve them, too!"

Maddy smiled.

Down the basement, Benny and Tucker were already engaged in playing a serious game of video football. They didn't dare play *Revenge of the Rabid Leprechauns*. That would have to wait until the others arrived. Tucker had a pretty good living arrangement. The family room was in the basement and that was where he played most of his video games. His bedroom was also down there, so he could kind of live in his own little world and cut himself off from the rest of the family. Except when Maddy would come down and bother him.

"Back to pass…looking…looking," came the voice from the game. "A deep pass down the right side with a man open…touchdown Vikings!"

Tucker jumped to his feet and did a dance.

"You are SO lucky! It was fourth and 23. There is no way you should have scored on that!" Benny shouted, punching his rolled-up sleeping bag.

"It's not luck, it's skill. Skill, baby, skill!" Tucker bragged.

"Luck, baby, luck!"

"As if!" Tucker said confidently.

About ten minutes later, they heard footsteps coming down the stairs. It was Josh and Crandal.

"Cranberry! The Josher! It's about time!" Tucker shouted.

He paused the game and he and Benny jumped to their feet and gave them high fives. Josh and Crandal couldn't have been more different. Crandal had hair that was gelled, mildly spiked, and dyed a few shades darker than its normal color. He liked to wear ragged jeans with rips in them, black shirts, and black cowboy boots. He sometimes was a bit more worldly and wise than his friends; his mother was a single woman who didn't like putting many restrictions on him. Tucker liked being around him most of the time. Crandal had a great sense of humor when things were going well. But he was also moody and had a dark side to him. His humor and tongue could become mean when things didn't go his way. Josh was usually the person who knocked him down a few pegs when he started crossing over the line and Crandal was usually smart enough to stop.

Josh wore black-rimmed glasses and combed his dark brown hair straight down over his forehead. His clothes were never fashionable and were probably hand-medowns from one of his older brothers. At first glance, one might even judge him to be a nerd. A few boys at school had made the mistake of judging him by his appearance, thinking that he looked like an easy target for teasing or bullying. They found out the hard way that is was better to be his friend than his enemy. Tucker had even seen Josh fight a middle-school boy when the kid wouldn't stop making fun of his glasses. Josh claimed he was so tough because he had a lot of practice fighting his older brothers. Tucker enjoyed having someone like Josh for a friend. He liked competing against him in different sports and he was also nice to have around if anyone from another neighborhood attempted to cause trouble. Josh would be the first one to jump in and stick up for one of his buddies.

"Are we ready to get down to business?" shouted Crandal. "Let's get this party started. Break out the Rabid 'Kons!"

"We can't play *Rabid Leprechauns*. Poodlehead isn't here yet," Benny said.

"Well, give Poodles a call and get him over here. We ain't got all night!" Crandal answered back.

"It's only five after seven. Let's give him a few more minutes," Tucker said.

"Poodles has ten minutes. If he's not here, I say we play," Crandal snapped. "We ain't got all night, Junior!" Junior, and sometimes Jackson were names Crandal liked to call people when he was feeling overconfident.

"Settle down, Grimy. We'll play when Poodlehead gets here," said Josh.

Crandal didn't like being called Grimy. He didn't mind "Cranberry" but not "Grimy." He also didn't like to be called "Beans." And he *really* hated it when anyone combined the two and called him "Grimy Beans," a play on his last name of Bino-Grimes.

"Okay, Junior, keep your shirt on. We'll wait," said Crandal, backing down. Crandal and Josh were able to join Benny and Tucker in playing the football game. Fifteen minutes later, Poodlehead came tromping down the stairs.

"Well, if it isn't me laddies playing a wee game of football!" Poodlehead shouted in his Irish accent as he entered the room.

"Glad you could finally make it, Poodlesheep. Our night is messed up waiting for you!" Crandal said with a bit of a bite in his tone.

"Relax, Grimy. He's only about fifteen minutes late," Josh said, sticking up for Poodlehead. It was the second time he'd called Crandal "Grimy" and Crandal got the message.

"Hey, I was just kidding, Poodles. C'mon in and let's get started!"

Poodlehead tossed his sleeping bag and backpack on the floor and joined the other boys.

"Snack time!" called a small voice from the stairway. It was Maddy coming down the stairs with bags of popcorn, followed by Mrs. McTeal carrying a pitcher of cherry-flavored drink. Mr. McTeal followed them. The boys paused the game.

Oh no, Tucker said in his head. *Maddy just never gives up.*

"It looks like you guys are set up for quite a night!" remarked Mr. McTeal, looking around the room.

"Looks like a lot of fun. I sure wish I could stay down here and play, too!" Maddy said, looking at her dad. Mr. McTeal chuckled. "I'm sure you would. But I have a feeling that Tucker and his friends don't feel the same way."

Phew! thought Tucker. He looked at his dad and smiled. He was glad that he understood.

"You guys sure spend a lot of time playing these games. And if it's not this, you're on the computer or the internet, and if it's not that, you're texting or playing a game on a cell phone. Don't you guys ever get tired of it?" Mrs. McTeal asked. Tucker chewed on the side of his lip. He hated it when she lectured him, but it was even worse when she lectured all his friends, too. He wished his mom would just drop off the snacks and leave and take Maddy with her.

"What is there to get tired of? I can't seem to get enough!" Crandal answered honestly. "I once played for over 24 hours straight last summer. I'd just got *Brouhaha at Shangri-La* and I started playing right after we got back from breakfast at Burger Busters. I even ate while I played and I only took bathroom breaks. I played all day and all night and beat the game by the next morning. My mom got so mad she said if I ever did that again she'd make me wait a whole week the next time I wanted a new game that came out." Tucker smiled, as did the others. Tucker thought Crandal might be exaggerating a little, but he also knew of Crandal's devotion and endurance when it came to non-stop gaming. It was legendary. He often felt that if his parents would give him a little more slack, he might be as good a gamer as Crandal.

Mr. McTeal smiled, but through the smile there was concern behind his eyes.

"Well, we're going to head upstairs and leave you guys alone. Tuck, try to hold it down to a dull roar down here." Fortunately, the McTeal floors were insulated well against noise so unless there was a small explosion in the basement, the boys wouldn't be disturbing anyone.

"I want you guys to be in bed at one o'clock at the very latest. That's more than fair. Oh and before you call it a night, can you let Bandit out to use the bathroom? He pulled out a bag of stale spicy hot chips we'd tossed in the trash and ate the whole thing. He's been smelling things up pretty good tonight. I think his stomach is a bit rumbly."

"Light a match. That's what my dad does when I stink it up," Poodlehead offered.

Tucker laughed. "No problem, Dad. I'll make sure to let him out."

Mr. McTeal punched Tucker playfully on his shoulder and headed upstairs. Mrs. McTeal turned to follow. "Goodnight, boys!" she said. "Have fun fighting those Rabbit Leprechauns!"

"*Rabid* Leprechauns!" Poodlehead shouted.

"Whatever," she answered.

"Mom, can I stay down here just for a few minutes to watch them play that new game?" Maddy asked.

"I don't see how that could hurt. You did do such a good job making that cherry drink for them."

Tucker shot Maddy a quick icy stare. Maddy smiled.

"You come up in about fifteen minutes," Mrs. McTeal said and headed upstairs. Tucker watched his mom walk to the top of the stairs and close the door. He was just about to chew into Maddy when she said, "Who wants popcorn?" and ran over to the table where the bags of popcorn were.

"I'll take a bag," said Poodlehead.

"Me too," added Crandal.

"I may as well have one, too," said Benny.

"I'll pass on it. I don't like popcorn sticking in my teeth," said Josh.

Maddy happily grabbed the bags and handed them out. This was driving Tucker nuts.

"Cherry drink? It's my specialty!"

They all thought it was a great idea. Everyone except Tucker, of course. Maddy poured each boy a glass and handed them out.

"Hey, what about *KaBlam!?*" he asked.

"We can drink this and *KaBlam!* I got plenty of room!" Benny said as he patted his stomach.

"Napkins?" she asked.

That was about all Tucker could stand.

"Aren't you about ready to leave?"

"Nope. Mom said I have fifteen minutes."

"It's okay, she ain't hurting anyone," offered Poodle-head.

Tucker had had enough.

"Really? Since when did she become your girlfriend?" He knew that was hitting low, but he felt it necessary to take action on this situation.

"Girlfriend…What…? No way… She is not…" Poodlehead's face was turning red.

"Maddy's pretty young for you, isn't she, Poodles?" Crandal asked. *Good old Crandal,* Tucker thought. He could always count on him to join in on teasing someone. Maddy would be running upstairs in embarrassment any second now. He could always make it right with Poodle-head later.

Maddy's smile left her face. She looked over at Poodlehead and then back to Tucker. She may have been younger than he was, but she was very quick to analyze a situation and then change things to her advantage.

"Did you say girlfriend? I know who Tucker would like to be *his* girlfriend!" The smile was back on her face.

All eyes quickly turned to Maddy and Tucker felt the air come out of the room. A while back, in a moment of weakness, he'd made the horrible mistake of telling Maddy of his longtime crush on Monique Duboise. He'd been in love with Monique since the first time he laid eyes on her in first grade. He felt his knees going weak. If it ever got out that he liked her, he'd never be able to look Monique in the face again. Tucker began to panic. And whenever he panicked his imagination would run wild. Like a movie, entire scenes would play out in his mind in seconds. In this movie, Tucker was wearing ragged clothes because he had quit school over the shame of everyone knowing of his love for Monique. Soon he was living as a hobo along the railroad tracks and eating beans out of a can, his life in ruins because he couldn't bear the thought of ever seeing Monique again. And it was all because of Maddy's big mouth.

Maddy looked over at Tucker. He swallowed hard. He felt like small bird being eyed by a cat.

4
THE END OF THE BEGINNING

MADDY PAUSED FOR a moment and smiled. Then she walked over and pulled a little brown bag off of the shelf.

What on earth is she doing? Tucker wondered. The bag was too small to hold the L.C. Webster yearbook and he hadn't hidden any pictures of Monique around the house.

She slowly reached into the bag. Tucker felt his mouth grow dry.

Out came the new *Revenge of the Rabid Leprechauns* game. She pointed to a beautiful blonde female leprechaun on the cover and giggled.

"Who?" Crandal laughed. "Tucker likes her? Fianna, the Leprechaun Princess? Give me a break. Every boy thinks she's a major babe."

Tucker let out a huge but silent sigh of relief

"Since you have it out, let's forget the football game and get started with some real leprechaun action!" Benny said.

The focus and the excitement about the new game had shifted the attention away from Tucker. He looked over at Maddy. He wasn't sure if he should be mad at her for scaring him to death or thankful for keeping his secret.

For now, he decided it would be much wiser to ignore her and let her stay her fifteen minutes without complaining.

Maddy had been gone for some time and the boys were now completely absorbed in the game.

"Oh wow!" shouted Poodlehead. "So the Rabid Leprechauns end up in a black hole and THAT'S how they end up encountering the Ninja Munchkins again! Of course, time travel! It makes perfect sense! Who would have ever guessed?"

"Yeah, a real shocker, isn't it?" Tucker answered with mock enthusiasm.

"Hey, I think it's time to break out the *KaBlam!*" Josh said. Poodlehead agreed and went over to the basement refrigerator and pulled out a red six-pack with an exploding stick of dynamite on each can that read, "'*KaBlam! Cola*, As much caffeine as the law allows!'"

"Drink up, me laddies," Poodlehead exclaimed. "We got some serious Ninja Munchkin tail to kick!"

They all banged their cans together in a toast with Poodlehead proclaiming, "Long live McCrud, the true and rightful Rabid Leprechaun king!" All the boys laughed at Poodlehead's toast, and his phony Irish accent made it even funnier. As the excitement and the intensity of the game progressed, the faster Tucker and the boys downed their cans of *KaBlam!* and munched away at the various candy bars they began pulling out of their backpacks. After about an hour, Poodlehead's can was empty.

"This little lamby wants more *KaBlamy!*" he announced. He went back over to the refrigerator and pulled out another six-pack of cans.

"This is on me!" he announced, giving everyone another can. Poodlehead, by nature, was always a bit wired, but *KaBlam! Cola* seemed to wind him up even more.

"To McCrud, long may his mouth foam!" the boys again laughed and touched their cans of *KaBlam! Cola* together in a toast.

The game went on and time flew by.

"The Insane Robot Assassins! No! They've betrayed us and we're getting wiped out like flies! I knew that the alliance with them was too good to last!" shouted Crandal as he frantically hit the buttons of his control, feverishly defending himself from the mechanical traitors.

"The Zombie Carp!" Josh shouted. "They're coming out of the ground everywhere! I can't shake them! This whole thing was a trap!"

"I'm going down, too!" Benny desperately cried, trying every move he could think of to escape.

"No! No! It can't end here! Not after getting this far! If we die here we'll be sent all the way back to the Cave of O'Leary's Doom!" Tucker howled in despair.

"Not on my watch!" Poodlehead announced dramatically. There was a cold determination in his voice. "No Zombie Carp or a bunch of tin cans are going to stop us from making it to the Ninja Munchkin Mountain!" His voice carried a hint of anger.

What happened next was almost beyond description and became a thing of legend in the neighborhood. The only explanation was that Poodlehead was so full of caffeine that it gave him some kind of superhuman powers. His fingers became a blur on his controller. His Rabid Leprechaun's shillelagh began to twirl and whirl at such an incredible speed that any Zombie Carp or Insane Robot Assassin near him had no chance at all and were being shattered into tiny pieces, like light bulbs being struck by a hammer. He then began to make a series of moves that none of the boys had ever seen before or had even believed possible. He then ran directly toward a group of Insane Robot Assassins.

"What are you doing, Poodlehead? Don't do that, it's certain death!" Tucker warned.

The Insane Robot Assassins aimed their guns at him. "Foolish leprechaun!" one of the robots shouted in a deep and sinister robotic voice. Then they all began to fire. There was no doubt in anyone's mind that the game was over. The Insane Robot Assassins were, well, just that—assassins. They never missed their targets. But Poodlehead's leprechaun began moving like a gymnast with his pants on fire! He flipped and rolled, bounced and cart-wheeled, all the while deflecting every shot with his shillelagh and closing in on the metal monsters.

Tucker was amazed. "That's impossible! That is literally impossible! No one's that fast!"

But Poodlehead was. He might never be able to do it again, but he was doing it now. Right before he reached the robots, he made a move no one even knew was in the game. He planted his shillelagh in the ground and pole vaulted high above them. When he was at the peak of his vault, he raised his shillelagh high above his head. To everyone's surprise (including Poodlehead's), a crackle of lightning came from the sky, which directly struck his shillelagh. There was a loud clap of thunder and Poodlehead's leprechaun shouted, "By the power of the Blarney Stone, I smite ye!" Froth began pouring out of his fierce-looking leprechaun mouth like foam from the top of a shaken bottle of soda. His shillelagh slammed down upon the robots. Another boom of thunder rang out and the Insane Robot Assassins were no more, disintegrating into a million tin pieces.

Poodlehead's shillelagh was glowing now and electricity began spitting out the top of it. The Zombie Carp had stopped attacking (which was incredibly fortunate since all the other players had been only seconds away from certain death) and the zombies desperately began attempting to burrow back into their underground homes. But Poodlehead was having none of that. He pointed his shillelagh at them and fingers of lightning shot out from his stick and attached themselves to each Zombie Carp. They could do nothing but flop around on the ground. The other players stared at the screen with their mouths hanging open in awe.

"Destroy the Zombie Carp before they recover!" Tucker shouted, bringing everyone back to their senses. Their shillelaghs made quick work of the helpless flopping fish. Moments later, all that was left were five Rabid Leprechauns. A door in a large tree magically opened and the five rabid heroes headed inside. They had made it to the next level.

There was complete silence for a moment. Benny finally proclaimed, "That was insane! I've never seen anything like that before in my life!"

"Excell-aun-tay, grome-ay-graun-tay!" Poodlehead mumbled with a dazed look in his eyes.

"Poodlestar, you are the man!" shouted Crandal. They paused the game and everyone gave Poodlehead high fives. They hoisted Poodlehead on to their shoulders, his head inches from the ceiling, and danced around the basement.

"How'd you do that, Poodles?" Tucker asked as they set him down.

"I have no idea, Tuck! It just came to me...I suddenly knew exactly what to do and I could do it faster than ever!"

"Dudes! I'll bet it was the *KaBlam!*" Crandal offered. "Maybe if we all drink another one, we can do what Poodles did."

Benny ran over and got the four remaining cans of *KaBlam! Cola* and a can of another brand of regular cola. "Someone's going to have to have to drink the baby soda."

"I will, since I already have the power," Poodlehead offered selflessly.

They popped opened their sodas. "To Poodlehead!" Josh shouted as they hit their cans together for another toast.

The game continued. Maybe it really was the *KaBlam! Cola*. Maybe it was only the belief that there was some kind of power from the *KaBlam! Cola*. Or maybe it was the rush they all got from watching the remarkable moves of Poodlehead. But the boys all seemed to play better than they had ever played before. They triumphed over Karate Clowns, scaled the Cliffs of Calamity, and defeated the Seven-Headed Weasel Dragon of Gobish Din. They were so absorbed in their video world that no one heard the whine and the scratching at the basement door of a frantic dog desperately needing to go outside.

"I'm getting hungry for some real food," Benny said. "I can't handle eating any more candy bars. Tucker, do you have anything in the basement fridge down here to munch on?"

"I don't know...Take a look."

Benny put his controller down and opened the refrigerator. There was fruit in the crisping drawer but not much else except condiments like ketchup and mustard and relish. He opened the freezer. Bingo! A thin-crust pizza!

"Hey, can we eat this pizza?"

"Yeah. Just toss it in the microwave."

"Are you insane? Microwave pizza? Yech! It comes out all soggy."

"Well, we don't have an oven down here."

"How about I go upstairs and bake it up there?"

"I don't know... I don't think they want us messing around..."

"C'mon, Jackson!" Crandal said. "I'm hungry, too. Let Benny pop in a pizza. I'll bet he's a good cook. Look at him, Tuck. He's a chubster. I'll bet Benny's made and eaten plenty of pizzas in his day."

"Yeah, I'm a good cook," Benny answered, not noticing the dig Crandal had made about his weight.

Tucker was trying to play the game. It was too difficult to think and play at the same time. His parents never said anything about not using the oven upstairs. What could it hurt?

"Okay, but be really quiet," he said. Then he and the others went back to the game.

Benny made his way up the stairs with the pizza and into the kitchen. Bandit was very happy to see someone come upstairs to finally let him out. He began excitedly jumping up and down at the back door.

"Bandit, my friend!" Benny whispered as he bent over. "Happy to see me, huh?" Bandit licked his hand and Benny patted his head and walked into the kitchen. Bandit whimpered and jumped at the back door. Benny was thinking too much about his pizza to notice. He walked over to the kitchen sink and turned on the little light above it. He held the package up to the light. "Heat oven to 350 degrees. Place pizza on oven rack. Bake for 25 minutes." Benny had never actually made a pizza before all by himself, but he had watched his older siblings make them many times. He turned the oven on, unwrapped the pizza and popped it into the oven. "Easy as pie…pizza pie!" he thought to himself and headed back downstairs. Benny went back to playing the game with the others while the pizza baked.

"I gotta take a break for a second. Keep playing without me!" Poodlehead said, getting up and leaving a bit later. He stopped to pull something out of his backpack.

A couple of minutes later he came running out of the bathroom.

"Look at me! Look at me! I'm a Rabid Leprechaun!" Poodlehead shouted with a crazed look in his eyes. Rivers of foam began pouring out of his mouth. He ran over to Crandal and grabbed his arm, pretending to chew on it.

"Dude! What are you doing? You're crazy!" Crandal said laughing and jumping back. "You're slobbering that stuff all over me!"

All the caffeine he'd consumed had really caught up with Poodlehead. He dramatically turned and began to chase the others who jumped up from the floor and began trying to get away as fast as they could so that they wouldn't be slobbered on by his foaming mouth. He was drooling and dripping everywhere. Everyone was running and laughing. The foam finally slowed down and he collapsed, laughing on the floor.

"Oh man, that was great! That worked better than I thought!"

"How'd you do that?" Tucker asked.

"I used these," he said, pulling a couple small packets from his pockets. "People take these tablets for heartburn or gut aches. They drop them in water and they bubble like crazy. So instead of putting them in water I just popped them in my mouth!"

"That is way cool!" said Josh. "Have you got any more?"

"You better believe it! My dad has tons of this stuff!" He went to his backpack and pulled out a whole box. The boys eagerly grabbed the packets. They ripped them open and then stood in a circle.

"One...two..." Poodlehead counted as they all held their tablets in their fingers, ready to pop them in their mouths.

"Hold it!" Tucker shouted. "If we're going to be Rabid Leprechauns we'll need shillelaghs!"

"Yeah, right," Josh said. "Where would we get shillelaghs?"

"I happen to just have some in the other room." Tucker ran over to a storage room and returned with a canvas bag full of shillelaghs.

"Pick your weapon!" he proudly said.

"Golf clubs! That's perfect!" Poodlehead exclaimed.

Each boy grabbed a club. They were all pumped up by the game, by the caffeine, by the thought of actually becoming a Rabid Leprechaun while the foam lasted.

"One..two...three...go!" Poodlehead shouted.

They all popped the tablets in their mouths. In a few seconds the foam started flowing and the chaos began. Poodlehead was so hyper by this time that he ran over and wacked Benny on the thigh. Benny grabbed his leg and yelped.

"Owww! Oh man, it is on!" he said as foam bubbled out of his mouth and he began chasing Poodlehead around the room. Tucker, Crandal and Josh began using their clubs like sabers, swinging and sword fighting each other. First Josh was sword fighting with Crandal, but then Tucker whacked Crandal from behind. When Crandal turned to engage Tucker, Josh took the opportunity to whack Tucker on the calf. Back and forth it went, getting wilder and crazier. Tucker had never felt so alive in his life. They weren't just playing *Rabid Leprechauns*, they *were* rabid leprechauns.

And then everything went wrong.

Benny and Poodlehead had been chasing each other while laughing hysterically and taking wild swings at one another. Benny came at Poodlehead just when Poodlehead decided to turn and chase Benny for a while. As he turned around to face Benny, Benny's putter caught poor Poodlehead directly in the mouth. There was the sound of a clink as metal met tooth and the foam turned red in Poodlehead's mouth and he let out a howl.

"My lip! My tooth!" He put his fingers in his mouth and grabbed his front tooth. It wiggled. At almost that same moment Tucker had taken a swing at Josh who dove out of the way. There was a loud pop. Tucker's club had missed Josh and went crashing right into the TV screen. The screen went black. Tucker gasped.

"EEEEEEEEEEEEEEE!"

The noise startled the boys.

"EEEEEEEEEEEEEEE!"

They all looked at each in confusion, holding their clubs in their hands (all except Poodlehead who was holding his mouth) while foam dripped from their mouths.

"EEEEEEEEEEEEEEE!" It was a smoke alarm.

"Why is that going off?" Tucker wondered in a panic.

"EEEEEEEEEEEEEEE!"

"Uh oh. I forgot about the pizza!" Benny said, his eyes open wide in horror.

"EEEEEEEEEEEEEE!"

5
THE SMELL OF BURNING POO
IN THE MORNING

"EEEEEEEEEEEEEEE!"

Mr. McTeal sat straight up in bed.

"EEEEEEEEEEEEEEE!"

"The smoke alarm!" he shouted as he leaped out of the bed.

"EEEEEEEEEEEEEEE!"

"The children!" Mrs. McTeal screamed. She threw the covers off and hit the floor running. She dashed toward the girls' rooms. Mr. McTeal ran toward the kitchen where he could smell smoke.

"What in the world?" Entering the kitchen, he flicked on the light and saw black smoke pouring out of the oven though the stove burners. He quickly grabbed the oven knob and flipped it off.

"Something must be in the oven!" He grabbed a couple of pot holders out of a drawer and pulled open the oven door. Smoke billowed into the kitchen. Inside the oven, he could see a flat object on the rack that was as black as a piece of charcoal. He grabbed a cooking pan and a metal spatula from a cabinet and hurried back to the oven. He shoveled the charred and smoking disc into the pan and then tossed it into the sink. As he turned the faucet handles, the water met the object with a loud hiss. Mr. McTeal looked around and took a deep breath. The crisis was over.

He hurried toward the back door to open a window and immediately felt his bare foot step in something mushy, cold, and slippery. Before he could stop his momentum, his other foot stepped in the same thing. His feet slipped out from under him and he fell right on his bottom. He looked on the floor and saw that he had slid in a rather large and sloppy pile that Bandit had deposited by the back door. The smell was horrible.

"Yuuuuuuuccccccckkkkkk!" he shouted.

"EEEEEEEEEEEEEEE!"

Mrs. McTeal came around the corner. The entire event had happened in just over thirty seconds. She had Olivia and Emily by the hands and Maddy was right behind them.

"What's that stench? It smells like burning poo in here!" she said over the screaming alarm. She looked down at the floor.

"My goodness, Ethan! Are you all right? How'd you end up on the floor?"

"EEEEEEEEEEEEEEE!"

"Yuuuuuuuccccccckkkkkk!" he shouted again. "My feet are covered in it!"

"Covered in what? What's going on? Where's the fire? Get down the basement and get Tucker!" She'd forgotten that the other boys were spending the night.

"EEEEEEEEEEEEEEE!"

Mr. McTeal turned and said, "Don't worry, I got it. Something was burning in the oven. It's in the sink now. Did you leave anything in the oven last night?" He looked down at his feet and shuddered.

"No, of course not. And how did the oven get turned on anyway?"

"EEEEEEEEEEEEEEE!"

"I have no idea. Grab me some paper towels, will ya? My feet are covered with a pile of poo that Bandit left near the door."

Mrs. McTeal tore some paper towels off the roller on the wall and tossed them to her husband. She put a chair under the smoke alarm, climbed atop it and pulled the battery out of the alarm, stopping the noise.

"I wanna go back to bed," said Olivia, who hadn't totally woken up yet.

"Me too," said Emily. Mrs. McTeal smiled and nodded. The girls walked sleepily back to their rooms.

"Yuck!" Mr. McTeal said again as he wiped off his feet. "What a way to start a Saturday!"

"I bet I know what happened. I bet they tried to bake something," Maddy said.

"Who? Who tried to bake something?" Mr. McTeal asked. But as soon as he asked the question, both he and Mrs. McTeal remembered about the sleepover.

"Of course! The sleepover!" said Mrs. McTeal, looking at her husband.

Mr. McTeal wiped off the rest of the mess as best as he could and got to his feet.

* * *

As they made their way quietly down the basement stairs, not a sound could be heard. Everything was dark and Mr. and Mrs. McTeal (and Maddy, who had followed them down) could hear the heavy breathing of the boys as they slept.

"Ouch!" said Mr. McTeal as he cried out in pain. He'd stepped on something hard with his bare foot. He grabbed the arch of his foot as a reaction and then reached down and picked up the offending object. It was a golf club. Specifically his putter and he had stepped right on the iron head. "Why in the world….?"

"What's wrong?" Mrs. McTeal whispered.

"I stepped on my golf club," he said, without whispering. "Turn on the lights."

The lights came on. There were candy wrappers everywhere and cans of *KaBlam! Cola* scattered all around the room. There appeared to be large wet puddles of something all over the carpet. Mr. McTeal's golf bag was lying in the middle of the floor and his golf clubs were all over the room. Some were bent and ruined. Mrs. McTeal gasped when she looked over and saw the hole and the crack in the middle of the TV screen.

"Get up!" Mr. McTeal ordered loudly.

Tucker had never been so scared in his life. As soon as the smoke alarm had sounded, he knew they had only one chance. There was no way he and his friends had time to clean up the mess, so Tucker hit the lights and told everyone to pretend to be asleep. If he'd been able to pull it off, he'd planned on cleaning things up before morning so it wouldn't look quite so bad. Maybe he could explain away the broken TV screen. But now they all had to face up to what they did and Tucker knew he was going to be held responsible. How did he let everything get so out of control? Why did the sleepover have to be at his house? He wished he could be anywhere else on the planet right now. The movie began playing in his head again. He saw himself living on some island far, far away. He was older, with a full beard and a mustache, for he had lived on the island for many years. Then he saw his parents and they looked worried and sad. "It was just a little mess. Why did we treat him so unfairly? I shouldn't have been so hard on him after that sleepover. It may have been a little untidy, but I had no right to yell the way I did," his father said. "No, it was my fault," his mother said. "I always favored the girls. No wonder he left and never came back."

"Get up!" Mr. McTeal shouted, stopping the movie in Tucker's head.

The boys got to their feet. By the tone of Mr. McTeal's voice, they figured it wouldn't help the situation if they pretended that they'd been sleeping. What did that matter anymore, anyway? They were caught and there was no way out.

"What in the world possessed you boys to do this? What did we ever do to deserve this?" he said, looking around the room. "For Pete's sake, it's six o'clock in the morning! You guys were supposed to end it at one o'clock. You never went to sleep, did you?" No one said a word.

Mr. McTeal looked at Tucker first. Their eyes met and for Tucker it was the worst feeling in the world. His dad's eyes held a mixture of anger and disappointment. His father shook his head. Tucker looked over at his mother and her eyes seemed to ask, "Why?" Her eyes left his as she looked around the room and then Tucker noticed that her face took on a look of alarm.

"My goodness gracious, Scotty! What happened to your mouth?"

Poodlehead's top lip had swollen to three times its size. It had taken on the appearance and size of a large red grape. There was blood all over his chin, neck and shirt. He tried to give her a sheepish smile and when he did his left front tooth fell out right onto the carpet.

"Snap," he said, looking down at the tooth.

6
JUDGMENT DAY

PARENTS WERE CALLED, and soon all the boys were gone. Poodlehead's dad took him directly to the dentist to see if his front tooth could be saved. Tucker sat alone in his bedroom after helping clean up the mess in the basement. He also had to clean up Bandit's mess because he didn't keep his promise to let Bandit out to use the bathroom. His parents were so angry with him that they barely said a word during that whole time. He'd never seen them this upset before. He'd made mistakes, but never this big. He could only sit and wonder what his punishment would be.

The next afternoon, all the parents met at Mac's Dinette, a little diner on the main street in the town of North St. Paul. A parents' meeting like this was something that Tucker was pretty sure had never happened before. All the boys knew something was brewing and they were all on edge. When Tucker's parents got home, they had a meeting with him in his bedroom.

"I don't have to tell you how disappointed we were with what went on here Friday night," Tucker's dad said, his voice sounding grim.

"It looks like Scotty has lost his front tooth. It was a permanent tooth. A permanent tooth! You boys also caused other damage that night. You know what it was," his mother added.

"We had a good talk with all the parents," his dad continued. "We discussed the concerns that we've all had recently. Concerns about how much time all of you boys spend playing video games or texting each other or posting things on those internet sites. You all seem to have stopped doing or thinking about anything else. You're all living in an artificial world—it's an awfully cheap imitation of the real thing. I don't care how good the graphics are. We just don't think it's very healthy."

Tucker felt bad about Scotty and his missing tooth but he wondered why his dad was telling him the other stuff. He never actually thought that things like rabid leprechauns and seven-headed weasel dragons were real.

"We parents talked about how these games were robbing you all of things that you can't get back again. Youth flies by pretty quickly. Once it is gone…" he paused, "It is gone for good."

Tucker still had no idea what his dad was talking about, but he kind of hoped that he kept focusing on it because it meant not having to deal with what happened Friday. Maybe he was going to get off easier than he thought.

"This is no way for you or your friends to live. It's a waste of your lives. That's why we all came to an agreement," Mrs. McTeal said. "Well, everyone except Mrs. Bino-Grimes."

Uh oh. Now Tucker was getting nervous. Hearing that parents were agreeing on something was probably not good. Probably not good at all.

"We've decided that starting today, all electronics are banned for the summer. That means no video games, no computer, no TV, and no cell phone."

Tucker felt the room begin to close in around him as he replayed the words in his head. *No video games...no computer...no TV...no cell phone.* He could feel the blood drain from his face. He was sure that this is what it felt like right before someone fainted.

"Mrs. Bino-Grimes thought this was too harsh and would not agree to it. We know how close you boys are with each other so we didn't want any of you to have the temptation of sneaking over to someone else's house and playing video games. So while Crandal can visit anyone he'd like, none of you can go inside his house. Do you understand?"

The news hit Tucker like a shillelagh over the head.

No video games...no computer...no TV...no cell phone. He couldn't concentrate on the other words that were coming out of his dad's mouth. No video games for the entire summer? What did he ever do to make his parents hate him? His suspicions had always been there. He'd long thought that they favored the girls over him and now this proved everything. He was also sure this devious plan that all the parents had agreed to had come from his dad and mom. They had talked the other parents into it. If only his parents were more like Crandal's mom. She wouldn't treat her son this way! His life was now ruined. He never even got to finish playing *Revenge of the Rabid Leprechauns!* How could he wait until September to find out how it ends? This was child abuse, pure and simple.

But since the disastrous sleepover had happened barely two days before, he didn't dare argue about it. But then he thought about it again. No video, no electronics. No nothing for the whole summer. He couldn't stop himself.

"Okay, how does this sound? I can still play for an hour a day if I…"

"Don't even start," his dad interrupted sternly. Tucker knew right away he had made a mistake even trying to see if there was any wiggle room. "That still doesn't let you off the hook for the damage done to the TV and golf clubs. You'll be working those off for some time. Do you understand?"

He nodded his head.

"I want to hear your answer," said his dad.

"Yes, I understand."

"Good."

His mom and dad got up and left the room. Sure, he'd made a mistake, he thought. Who hadn't? But to take away his games and all electronics for the entire summer? That was crazy! The more he thought about it, the angrier he became. He decided to do what he normally did when he couldn't handle life anymore. He laid face down on the bed and began screaming and shouting at the top of his lungs into his pillow. He began telling off the whole world. His feet began kicking the bed as if he were in a pool swimming. Occasionally he'd throw a punch into the pillow. He had worked himself into such a rage that he also began biting his pillow, biting it hard and shaking his head back and forth like a dog shaking a pull-toy. He was having one good-old-fashioned-feel-sorry-for-yourself temper tantrum.

"What in the world are you doing?" asked a small voice.

Tucker stopped his tantrum in mid-bite. He'd been enjoying his tantrum so much he hadn't heard anyone come into his room.

"Get out," his muffled voice said into his pillow.

"What?"

"You heard me, get out of here."

"It's very hard to hear someone when they talk into a pillow, you know."

Tucker lifted his face from the pillow and repeated himself.

"Whoa! Your face is really red and puffy. You kind of look like a monster or something."

Tucker let his face fall back into the pillow. He had no energy to even argue with Maddy at the moment. His life was over.

7
A CRAZY RIDE IN A KOOKY KASTLE

"SO WHADDYA THINK?" Poodlehead asked. His left front tooth was gone and he gave Tucker a big grin. "Pretty cool, huh?" Much of the swelling had gone down on his lip, but his smile was still a bit lopsided.

"Boy, I don't know. That's a pretty big gap you have there."

"I know! I can stick a pencil in it! Dr Ziemer said it'll be a few days until I get a fake tooth."

It had been a couple of days since the boys were given the devastating news about the video game ban. All of them were banned, of course, except for Crandal.

Tucker and Poodlehead had decided to ride their bikes to the World-O-Fun Park to meet Benny and Josh. Crandal's mother had gone out and purchased *Revenge of the Rabid Leprechauns* for him and he was too eager to play more of the game, so he chose to stay home. But Crandal did not go unpunished. He was banned from playing video games after ten o'clock in the evening for one week. But everyone knew even that would not be strictly enforced because Crandal's mom never followed through on punishing Crandal.

World-O-Fun was a small arcade and amusement park in town that was about a mile from all of their houses. It was not far from Mac's Dinette where their parents had the big meeting. While the park had a couple of garage-type buildings that housed video games, it also had a mini-golf course, a go-cart track, and an inflatable structure that kids jumped around inside called the Kooky Kastle. The boys had been specifically warned not to go in the video game buildings and they had all promised not to enter them. The only exception was that they could pass through one of the buildings so they could have access to the mini-golf course. If they broke their promise and played any arcade games, they'd be banned all summer from World-O-Fun, too. Tucker's dad was friends with Wild Bill Schiff, the owner of the park. As an added precaution, he had explained the situation to Wild Bill and the owner promised he'd put the word out to his employees to keep the boys away from the games.

Tucker and Poodlehead pulled their bikes up to the farthest building on the tar lot where the mini-golf course was. Benny's and Josh's bikes were already parked there.

"Hey guys, look at this!" Poodlehead said upon seeing Benny and Josh. He proudly pointed to the gap in his teeth.

Benny still felt terrible about the whole thing and cringed when he saw Poodlehead's mouth. Even though it was an accident, he still felt guilty. Benny's dad was furious and told Mr. Nova that he would pay for anything that wasn't covered. Even though he knew it had been an accident, Mr. Xiong had no time for foolishness and he

53

was angered and disgusted with how it all had happened. "If you act like fool, foolish things happen," he said.

"Nice," remarked Josh, looking at the gap between his teeth. "It makes you look like a genius, Poodles!" Poodlehead crossed his eyes and gave Josh a huge goofy smile.

They entered the building to pay for their mini-golf and an older boy was working behind the counter.

"Stay away from the games," he said with a smirk. The boys ignored his comment, paid for their tickets and headed outside to the course. When they got to the ninth hole, there was a wooden leprechaun cutout holding a pot of gold. The figure would set the pot down and pick it up again. Golfers had to time their putt so that the leprechaun wouldn't block the ball. Tucker looked at the face of the smiling figure and sighed.

"Remind you of anyone?" he asked. Benny looked at the bearded elf and grinned. For just a brief moment, he started to pretend his club was a shillelagh. He began to hoist it into the air and was going to shout, "By the power of the Blarney Stone, I smite ye!" but caught himself. He looked over at Poodlehead's gaping space between his front teeth. He sheepishly lowered his club.

As the group played on, dark clouds formed in the distance and a weak breeze blew. It felt good to be outside enjoying an early summer day. After finishing the eighteenth hole and figuring out the scores, Josh had low score and was proclaimed the winner. They decided to head for the go-carts next. They bought their tickets and a teenager who worked at the booth pointed them toward the correct gate.

"Nice teeth, Poodlehead," he commented as they walked by. "Oh, and by the way," he added with a sneering smile on his face, "you guys stay away from the video games."

"As if," Tucker muttered to himself. It was bad enough, he thought, that they couldn't play video games all summer. But why did his dad have to make it even worse by having the owner go and tell all the workers?

They all ignored the comments of the employee and hopped into the go-carts. The wind slapped at their faces as they all held their pedals to the floor and whizzed around the tar track. As Tucker skidded around the corners, he could hear the air whistling loudly in his ears. Louder than he'd ever heard. He felt proud of the noise because it meant he must really be burning up the track. But the wind he heard wasn't because he was going any faster; there was a summer storm brewing and it was moving their way. After about ten minutes, they were flagged down and instructed to drive their go-carts into the pit area. As they climbed out of the carts, they noticed that the sky had grown darker and the wind had increased.

"We still have time for the Kooky Kastle! Hurry up!" shouted Benny, looking at the darkening sky.

"Yeah, we hafta hit that before we go!" agreed Poodlehead.

The Kooky Kastle was a large inflated building made to look like a European castle. It had multicolored towers and doors and the windows were covered with white netting. Tucker and Josh didn't care much for the Kooky Kastle anymore. They'd started to notice that they were older and larger than most of the kids who went jumping and bouncing around inside of it. Perhaps since Poodle-head and Benny were short for their age, they hadn't noticed.

The park was never very busy on early summer week-day afternoons and the approaching storm had emptied out many of the customers who had been there. There was no one in the Kooky Kastle now except for a rather heavy-set girl who appeared to be about twelve years old. She was a bit of an odd-looking individual. She had pale white skin and wore shorts and a t-shirt that were too small. Her red frizzy hair was parted in the middle and then weaved into two long pigtails. For her size, she was actually pretty coordinated and Tucker was a bit fascinated watching her leap and bounce around, her pigtails flopping up and down and to and fro. Benny and Poodlehead bought tick-ets from the same boy who sold them at the go-cart rides and then they scrambled inside.

"C'mon in!" Poodlehead shouted to Josh and Tucker as he, Benny, and the big girl bounced happily around.

"We'll take a pass on this one," Josh shouted back.

Poodlehead did a seat drop and shouted, "Your loss!"

Tucker glanced up at the sky and he didn't like the looks of it. It already appeared darker than when they'd raced the go-carts just a few minutes before. The wind seemed to be picking up a bit, too. He noticed trees were starting to sway back and forth and he thought they should probably be on their bikes heading for home. He didn't like riding his bike in the rain. A few years ago when he was biking in a rainstorm, a bolt of lightning hit the street about thirty feet in front of him. The flash was so bright and the boom so loud, he fell off his bike and onto the street. He hadn't been hurt badly, but he always worried about being struck by lightning ever since that had happened.

Then as if someone had flipped a switch, the strength of the wind at the park increased dramatically.

"Wow, it feels like someone just started blasting us with a leaf blower!" Josh shouted. The sudden gust actually pushed Tucker back a step. Then his eyes grew wide. He was surprised to see the inflated building starting to lift up off the ground.

Poodlehead was the first to feel the building rise and he looked out the netted window. He looked down at the ground and noticed how the Kooky Kastle had actually risen a few feet into the air. He looked at Tucker and Josh.

"Excell-aun-tay, grome-ay-graun-tay!" he exclaimed with a big gaped-tooth smile and went back to bouncing. Seconds later, the North St. Paul storm siren sounded.

"C'mon you guys, you have to get out of there. There's a storm coming," shouted the boy working the ride. Tucker wondered why he'd waited so long to get them out. But it didn't matter anymore because that last gust of wind was nothing compared to what hit next. The next blast hit the Kooky Kastle hard and tilted it on its side. Benny, Poodlehead, and then the large red-headed girl went tumbling into a heap in one corner, with the girl landing on top of Benny and Poodlehead. The girl began screaming and crying and Poodlehead shouted out that she had landed on his neck. Benny yelled something in Hmong.

"Get out, get out!" yelled the panicked teen worker as he attempted to grab the doorway and hold it open. But the unstable building now blew back the other way, throwing the teen employee to the ground and tossing the three inside it to the other side. Tucker and Josh also tried to grab hold of the castle, but they were no match for a castle that had become a huge bucking bronco and they were tossed aside also.

"I wanna get out!" screamed the girl.

Employees of the park soon heard the screams and realized what was going on. They ran toward the Kooky Kastle to give their assistance. It was then that Benny had an idea. He scrambled to his feet and slipped his fingers through the white netting that served as windows for the building.

"Put your fingers through the netting and hold on like me!" he called out. Poodlehead and the girl saw what Benny had done and did the same. The Kooky Kastle began to twist and turn and swing and sway back and forth as it was buffeted by the wind, but at least the three were not being tossed around like ragdolls anymore. The other employees were only seconds away now and probably would have been able to hold the building down enough for the three to escape from their wild ride. But even stronger gusts of wind hit the building and then there was a loud ripping sound. The tube connecting the building to the machine that inflated it had torn away from its connection. Now there was nothing at all keeping the building attached to the ground. Tucker could hardly believe his eyes. In one swift movement, the building went soaring thirty feet up like some kind of hot air balloon. He caught a momentary glimpse of the faces of Poodlehead and Benny.

"Kuv tsis ntseeg tias yuav zoo li no!" shouted Benny in Hmong.

Poodlehead had a strange combination of fear and excitement on his face. It was frozen in a kind of horrified open-mouthed smile.

There was nothing now that Tucker, Josh, or the workers of World-O-Fun could do but watch the Kooky Kastle and its three reluctant airborne passengers shoot away from them into the ever-increasing distance.

The wind pushed the craft east. Through incredible luck or divine intervention the building-turned-airship stayed fairly upright in the wicked winds, remaining between twenty and thirty feet in the air.

"Run!" Tucker shouted to Josh. "Run like you've never run before!"

The boys headed after the Kooky Kastle, but they were stunned at how fast it was traveling away from them. They were near their bikes, so they quickly hopped on them and gave chase. Some of the World-O-Fun employees were on their cell phones calling 911. Others started running after their escaped building that held their customers hostage.

In the Kooky Kastle, the girl let out a long, high-pitched scream. Then with her white knuckles clutching the netting and her eyes shut tight, she took another deep breath and screeched some more. Benny was just concentrating on holding onto the netting and trying to ignore the hysterical screams of the girl. Poodlehead's mind was racing.

While he was certainly scared and worried, a part of him was actually enjoying this bizarre situation. It almost felt like he was in his own video game. When he thought of it that way, it didn't seem so bad. What were his options? There was certainly no way that he could steer or direct the path of the castle that he could think of. Could he escape? Maybe. He looked over at the doorway. Right now they were too high up to jump out of the door. But what if the wind carried them closer to the ground? Should he try to make it out the door? He was convinced that he should. What would happen to Benny? Would he be able to do it, too? He couldn't even begin to think about the screaming red-headed girl at this moment. Poodlehead would never have to deal with those questions because his ride was soon coming to an end. They were headed directly toward some electrical lines.

8
THE RESCUED AND THE RESCUERS

JOSH AND TUCKER could only watch what happened from their bikes. The Kooky Kastle had been racing east alongside Highway 36. Fortunately, there were few obstructions or buildings to block their path. But they could see the three travelers heading straight for the electrical wires that ran north and south across the highway. What happened next was incredible. Another gust of wind lifted the floating building up at the last second, which caused it to rise above the wires. But it grazed the top of one of the wooden support poles and the bump sent the building spinning in circles like a floating merry-go-round. Tucker and Josh peddled faster down the frontage road as they tried to catch up.

Poodlehead's only plan, as farfetched as it was, was now not even an option. With the castle spinning in circles, there would be no way that he could make it over to the doorway and escape. But he didn't have to think of another strategy because the Kooky Kastle suddenly came to a jerking halt. The stop had been so sudden that they were all ripped from their hold on the netting. They were again tossed into a corner—first Benny, then Poodlehead,

61

and then the screaming girl, who landed again right on top of Poodlehead.

Josh and Tucker slammed on the brakes of their bikes, slid sideways to a stop and hopped off. They both were walking toward the Kooky Kastle with their mouths hanging open. "No way! Absolutely, no way! What are the odds of that?" Tucker muttered. "Benny! Poodlehead! Are you guys okay up there?"

After the Kooky Kastle careened off the top of the pole, it continued east along the highway, spinning round and round as it traveled over Margaret Street. As fate would have it, in their path just fifty yards away was one of the most remarkable manmade creations in the world. Standing tall and proud was the city's celebrated landmark—the world's largest snowman. The concrete giant wore a black stove pipe hat and red scarf.

One of his enormous stick arms miraculously snagged the netting on the inflatable castle. It was the most incredible thing they'd all ever seen or experienced. Tucker later admitted that it was much more exciting than any video game he'd ever played.

The castle now hung from the snowman's outstretched left arm. The famous grinning giant appeared to be so proud of this most unlikely catch that if he'd been able to tip his stovetop hat, he would have. The Kooky Kastle's traveling days were over and now the question was how its passengers had fared.

"What happened? How are we hanging in mid-air?" shouted Poodlehead, poking his face up against the netting. Some of the air had gone out of the building now and it was beginning to look more like a huge deflated party balloon than a Kooky Kastle. The wind was still blowing and it rocked the hanging castle back and forth.

Tucker shouted up to Poodlehead that they were hanging from the arm of the town snowman and then he asked about the others. Benny put his face next to Poodlehead's and shouted out that he was fine.

"I don't know about the girl. I kinda think she fainted."

Soon the sounds of police and fire truck sirens could be heard. It was easy to hear them as they raced out from their buildings because both stations were only a block away. A police car made it first to the scene and in the car was Sergeant Veid Muiznieks (or Sergeant Veid, which he preferred to be called since only his mother could pronounce his last name properly), a 25-year veteran of the force. The car came to a screeching halt and Veid, despite his advancing age, leapt catlike out of the car.

"We just got the call," Sergeant Veid explained to Josh and Tucker. "Are your friends still in there?" he said, looking up at the snowman. "Are they okay?"

"We're okay," shouted Poodlehead. "Except the girl just woke up and by the look on her face, I think she's going to start screaming again."

"Okay, I can see you," Sergeant Veid said, stroking his overly healthy grey mustache and realizing that at the moment there wasn't a lot he could do. "Just hang tight. We'll get a fire truck to get you down."

Tucker and Josh were placed safely in his squad car and watched everything from the back seat. Moments later, a TV crew showed up. Then another car came from the local paper and they started taking pictures. There had been occasional drops of rain, but now it started coming down fairly strong. A fire truck with a ladder came on the scene. A fireman by the name of Berger was sent scrambling quickly up the ladder. Firefighter Berger cut the netting with some sort of utility knife, pulled the three out one at a time and carried them down the ladder. Poodlehead waved bravely at the camera with a big goofy smile on his face.

"Is this going to be on the news?" he asked.

The storm soon left as dramatically as it had come and within a couple of hours it was bright and sunny again, almost as if it had never happened. But the quick-moving storm had been fairly serious. Tucker heard later that a funnel cloud had been spotted in Lake Elmo, just a few miles east of North St. Paul and there were reports of trees down all over the area.

Benny, Poodlehead, and the girl (whose name, everyone discovered that evening while watching the news, was Agnes Frosniper) were whisked away and taken to a local hospital for observation. Miraculously, except for a few bruises, the only injury was to Poodlehead, whose neck was hurt when Agnes fell on him. The story made the local section of the daily paper the next day with the headline, "Kids Travel in Flying Building But Fail to Land in Oz." The picture below the headline showed

Poodlehead waving to the camera as he was carried down the ladder by firefighter Berger.

Early the next morning, Tucker, Josh, Benny, and Poodlehead headed over to Crandal's house to catch him up on the events of the day before. Crandal came out of the back door looking half-asleep. He'd been up late attempting to beat *Revenge of the Rabid Leprechauns*.

"I heard about what happened," he said, stretching his arms up into the sky and then giving out a loud yawn. "Sounded pretty awesome." He looked over at Poodlehead.

"What are you supposed to be, Poodlehead, a pirate or something?"

Poodlehead was quite a sight. Now, along with his missing front tooth, his right shoulder was hunched up near his neck. His white curly-haired head was also leaning a bit toward that shoulder.

"My neck is stiff from yesterday and I can't move it. The doctor says it will take a while for the muscles in my neck to relax. It feels better in this position."

"Well, all you need now is a parrot on your shoulder," Crandal said with a laugh. "I heard your neck got hurt when your fat girlfriend fell on you."

"Give me a break, Grimy. She wasn't my girlfriend. I didn't even know who she was."

"That's not what I heard!" he said, wiggling his eyebrows up and down and snickering. Leave it to Crandal, thought Tucker, to ruin something cool with his big mouth.

"Man, I was up late last night playing *Rabid Leprechauns*. But I suppose you guys wouldn't want to hear about that," he said, trying to sound compassionate, but there was a hint of a smile on his face. Crandal could never pass up a chance to rub something in.

"Why would we want to hear about it? You know we can't play it until September," Josh said with a bit of anger in his voice. "We're trying to make the best of a bad situation."

"Back off, Jackson, back off. I know."

"We're headed for Northwood Park. We heard there were some trees knocked down. You want to come with us?" Benny asked.

"Yeah, I heard that, too. I have to eat breakfast. I'll meet you guys down there in a bit." He looked at Poodlehead one more time. "Arrrrrr! See you in a little while, mateys!" he said in a pirate voice.

"If only you were half as funny as you think you are, maybe I'd laugh." Poodlehead shot back.

Crandal chuckled to himself and went back into the house.

"He's such a loser sometimes," Poodlehead said.

"Never mind him, Scotty," Josh said. "Let's go see what happened at the park." Calling Poodlehead by his birth name was Josh's way of trying to make him feel better.

Northwood Park was a small park just a couple of blocks away. It had a playground with a giant crooked slide along with the other standard park items like monkey bars, a merry-go-round and a swing set. It also had a baseball field, a basketball court and an outdoor hockey rink with a warming house that was formerly a railroad car. At the edge of the north end of the park stood a light blue water tower with a picture of North St. Paul's famous World's Largest Snowman painted on it. To the east of the park was a field which some said had been a pasture many years back. Just past the field was a small patch of woods that everyone called Cowern Woods because Cowern School was on the other side of the woods. There was only one road that led to the park, but it was a dead end so it was pretty private. The boys used to spend most of their free time at the park, but as they were growing older and other things caught their time and attention they spent less and less time there. Tucker couldn't remember the last time they'd been down there all together.

They soon came over the hill and rounded the corner to the park.

"Snap! Look at that!" said Poodlehead. "What a mess!"

There were leaves and branches on the ground everywhere. One large oak tree that was near the water tower looked like someone had taken a huge axe and divided it right down the center. The tree had split in half; one part was still upright and the other half was on the ground. Another tree near the warming house had fallen over completely, with its roots sticking up in the air. For some reason when Tucker looked at it, he felt a bit sorry for it. Trees always looked so strong and majestic. Somehow with its roots sticking up in the air like that, it looked undignified. Like a turtle on its back with its legs in the air.

The boys hopped on the part of the split tree that was lying on the ground and attempted to walk down it without falling off. If they fell off, they had to start at the beginning again. All of them were attempting to scale it except Poodlehead, who wasn't able to hold his arms out to balance on the tree on account of his stiff neck. He decided to walk through some of the fallen branches and leaves and try to kick them off as he walked. Tucker was just about to be the first one to make it all the way across the tree when he saw something move under a bunch of leaves and branches. The sudden movement that caught his eye surprised him so much that he lost his balance and fell off the downed part of the tree.

"What was that?" he shouted. "I saw something move under these leaves over there!"

He picked up a stick from the ground for protection. So did the others.

"It was right over here!" he said, pointing his stick in the direction of the spot where he saw it move.

"Maybe it's a raccoon!" Poodlehead said.

They formed a circle and began moving toward the area Tucker had pointed out, hitting the branches with their sticks. Suddenly a figure came bursting out of the branches, screaming like it was possessed.

"Ntuj es!" hollered Benny in Hmong. "It's Evil Caesar!" All the boys dropped their sticks and ran for their lives.

Every kid in the neighborhood knew who Evil Caesar was. He was a legend in the area, seldom seen but always feared. Caesar was the biggest, meanest cat you could ever imagine. He was dirty grey with black stripes covering his body and what looked like a black letter "M" on his forehead. On dark nights, children would tell bloodcurdling stories about ghosts, zombies, and Evil Caesar. Some said that the "M" stood for Monster or Mutant or even Murder. No one knew where he came from or exactly where he lived. Some claimed that he was half bobcat. Tucker's dad had told him that Evil Caesar was something called a feral cat. He said a feral cat is a kind of house cat that had no owner and then becomes wild. No one knew how the big cat got his name or how he came to be wild, but everyone knew that he didn't like people, or much of anything else for that matter.

Evil Caesar's back was arched and he let out a yowl that sent shivers down all of the boys' spines. His ears were pinned back and he flashed his teeth. His eyes burned like fire. He had been disturbed while he was hunting and he was spitting angry. The boys stopped running when they got about a hundred feet away and turned around to look at him. His eyes locked on their eyes and he let out another howl of rage at them.

"Get out of here, you devil!" shouted Benny. Josh picked up a big stick and threw it. It went cart-wheeling through the air and landed a few feet from the cat. Evil Caesar hissed again and glared at the boys. He was clearly uncomfortable being this visible and so out in the open. Reluctantly, he began to back up. He slowly turned his back to them and then dashed away across the road and into some deep weeds in the field.

"I can't believe it! Evil Caesar! That was Evil Caesar, man!" shouted Benny, acting like he'd just seen a celebrity. "I'd heard about him for all these years, but I'd never seen him before!" His hands were shaking.

"That's the second time I've seen him," said Poodlehead. "A couple years ago, me and Josh saw him drag a big ol' jackrabbit into some weeds by the swamp. Remember that Josh?"

"Yep," Josh replied. "He looks even bigger and meaner than I remember!"

"I saw him once late last winter," said Tucker. "We heard some really scary howling sounds in the backyard late one night. My dad got a flashlight and saw him sitting on top of our fence. He hissed when the light shone on him and then he disappeared. My dad said he thought he was looking for a mate. I could tell he made even my dad nervous."

The boys walked back to the place where Evil Caesar had jumped out at them. Tucker saw some black feathers on top of the leaves and branches and when he cleared the branches away he saw a dead crow that Evil Caesar had killed and was starting to eat.

"Oh man, look at this!" he shouted to the others. Benny, Poodlehead, and Josh hurried over to take a look at Evil Caesar's work. "No wonder he was so ticked off!"

But then they heard some rustling sounds and saw some movement under the branches and leaves. Clearing it away, they saw sections of a large nest that appeared to have been destroyed when the tree fell. But near the nest were two young crows with just a light covering of feathers on them. They were actually quite large and plump for being so young; they were about the size of Tucker's fists.

"Awesome!" shouted Poodlehead. "I've never in my life seen baby crows before!" The two young crows tried to waddle away underneath some leaves and branches to hide, but Tucker reached out and grabbed one and Josh grabbed the other. The two crows squawked in terror.

"Hey, don't worry little guy, we're not going to hurt you," he said, holding the crow with both hands near his chest. Josh did the same.

"I wonder if there are any more?" Poodlehead asked. "Maybe not," he said, answering his own question. "If Evil Caesar has been here very long, they might be dead."

It was now clear to the boys what had happened. When the tree split in half, the nest and the baby crows had fallen from the tree. The mother had bravely tried to protect her young from the monstrous cat and had died trying.

"Here's another one!" Benny shouted as he picked it up. Poodlehead was looking too, but his stiff neck and shoulder prevented him from moving as quickly as he liked. But a few minutes later, he also found one hiding beneath the branches. The poor birds were frantically squawking, more than likely thinking that they were going to be eaten. The boys searched for another fifteen minutes, but it appeared that the nest had contained just the four baby crows.

"What are we going to do now? We can't leave them here. Who would know anything about baby crows?" Benny wondered.

Tucker smiled. "I know just the person!"

9
THE WORST SUMMER EVER

TUCKER LIVED CLOSEST to the park, so they headed there. As they came to his house, Maddy was sitting on the cement driveway drawing pictures with chalk. She heard them coming and saw that each one of them was holding something.

"What have you guys got?" she asked. As they came closer, she could see it was some sort of animal. "That is so cool!" she squealed. "What are they?" With all the excitement of finding the birds, Tucker actually answered his sister's question without sounding angry. As he explained about the fallen tree in the park, Evil Caesar, and the dead mother bird, Mrs. McTeal came out the back door. The window had been open and she had heard the whole thing.

"They are so cute!" Maddy said, grinning as she got up off the cement. "Can I pet it?"

"Why don't we wait on that," Mrs. McTeal said. "I'm sure they are scared to death as it is and any more hands on them will just frighten them more. Maddy, why don't you go down the basement and get a box that we can put the crow in. Also grab an old towel I tossed in the rag box." Maddy, who loved nothing better than to help, dashed into the house.

"So what are your plans?" Mrs. McTeal asked.

"I guess we don't have any. We just wanted to save them from Evil Caesar."

Mrs. McTeal couldn't argue with that. She knew full well the cat's fierce reputation. Even the thought of Evil Caesar sent chills up her spine. "Do you even know what they eat?"

"Probably worms," said Poodlehead confidently.

Maddy came out the door with a small box and a faded blue hand towel. Mrs. McTeal placed the towel in the box and formed it into the shape of a nest. "Why don't you try putting the bird in there?" Tucker carefully set the bird in the towel.

"You're a good nest builder, Mom!" Maddy said. The baby crow seemed a bit more comfortable not being in the hands of a human.

"I was thinking that Mrs. Field might know what to do. She seems to know a lot about nature and animals," Tucker said.

"You know, that's not a bad idea," Mrs. McTeal said. "Let me give her a call and see if she's home." She went inside.

While they waited, the other boys put the birds they were holding down together in the grass. The baby crows huddled together, squawking, looking confused and frightened. The kids could hear Mrs. McTeal on the phone, but they couldn't hear what she was saying. After about a half hour, she came back out.

"Well, I spoke with Mrs. Field. After I told her what happened, she made a few phone calls and called me back. She contacted different state agencies and people she knew who deal with stray and orphaned animals. Because of the storms that blew through the area yesterday, they have been swamped with calls, especially for young birds. None of them have the room to take anything in. Technically, it's against the law to take in any wild animal, so they suggested that you leave the birds where you found them."

"That's crazy! We can't do that! You know what would happen if we would put them back!" said Tucker.

"You're right," said Mrs. McTeal. "They don't know the circumstances here. Sometimes you just have to do the right thing and this is one of those times. I'd already come to that conclusion, as did Mrs. Field. She was fully aware of Evil Caesar's reputation and what would happen if you put them back. She said that's why she thought it'd be a good idea for you to pay her a visit."

"What are we gonna do with our crows if we all go over there?" asked Josh.

"For the time being, why don't you guys bring them to your homes and find boxes and towels for them," Tucker said. "I'll ride my bike over to Mrs. Field's house and see what she says and I'll come back and tell you."

The boys couldn't think of a better plan. The box that Maddy had brought up was too small for more than one bird and the truth was that they also wanted to show off the crows and tell anyone who would listen about their dramatic encounter with Evil Caesar.

"I'll take good care of it when you're gone," assured Maddy.

"Okay..." Tucker said, feeling a bit uncertain about the arrangement. "Just don't mess with it. Mom, will you watch her?"

"It'll be just fine. Go."

Tucker hopped on his bike and the boys headed off to their homes.

When Tucker pulled up to her house, Mrs. Field was out in the front yard working in her flower garden. She had on a big floppy gardening hat and grey gloves. She had the longest hair Tucker had ever seen and she kept it braided in a single pony tail that ran down her back.

"Well, look what the cat dragged in," she said with a laugh. "How you doing, Kiddo?" she asked, pulling herself up to her feet. She wiped her forehead and adjusted her glasses. "You guys are having quite the start to your summer. I saw Scotty and Benny on the news last night! First you and your buddies take a ride in the sky in the Crazy Castle and the very next day you take on Supercat and end up with a bunch of baby birds. What are your plans for tomorrow? You gonna capture Bigfoot or something?"

Tucker laughed. It was called the Kooky Kastle and *he* hadn't actually ridden in it, but he figured she knew all that already. She liked to tease him and he never minded.

"I heard about your problem and I think I just might be able to help you out. C'mon in the house for minute." She brought him into her office and sat down at her computer.

"I know a little bit about crows, but I also did some quick internet searches on what they eat and how often to feed them. I printed it out for you. I figured that's the most important thing you boys need to know right now. Are you ready?"

"Sure."

"They're hungry little buggers. They need to be fed about every half hour."

"What? As if! I have to feed it every thirty minutes?"

"That's right. That's why you were one of my prized students. Thirty minutes equal a half hour," she said, smiling a bit. "You up for the job?"

How would anyone be able to do that? That meant that he'd be feeding his crow 24 hours a day. He was really starting to regret ever coming across them and bringing them home. If only his parents hadn't freaked out over what happened at the sleepover, he'd be playing *Rabid Leprechauns* right now and not having to deal with this mess.

"Here's the good news," she said. "After a couple weeks, they start to need food less often, so if you can hang in there, you might make it."

Losing out on video games over the summer *and* having to babysit crows? Tucker decided right then and there to put an end to the insanity.

"Mrs. Field, this isn't going to work. No way am I digging up worms all day. I don't have money to buy worms, either. Do you know how much they cost at a bait shop? Your friends at those animal shelters are just going to have to take the crows."

"Tucker, you know there is no room."

"That's not my problem."

"So, you're going to let them starve or let Evil Caesar eat them?"

Tucker hated that she had put it that way. It made him feel like a horrible person.

"Yeah. I guess so. It's not my fault that there was a storm." He turned and started walking toward the door. His anger about his ruined summer was stronger than any feelings of guilt he had about the death of some stupid baby birds.

Mrs. Field could see that Tucker was serious. "Tucker McTeal, you hear me out. It may not be as bad as you think. Crows are omnivores. You remember what that means from our science classes?"

"Sure. That means they eat just about everything."

"I wouldn't want you and your buddies spending the whole summer digging holes or going broke. There is something out there for them to eat that is cheap and easy to buy. In fact, you probably have some of this stuff in your house."

"What is it?"

"Canned dog food. Crows evidently love it and it's very good for them. For the next two weeks, throw in a crushed-up hard-boiled egg in it, shell and all—the calcium's good for their bones."

Tucker had plenty of dog food at his house, but at the moment it didn't really matter to him whether they ate worms or dog food. Crushed-up eggs? As if. He didn't want the responsibility. Tucker's mind wandered. Wasn't it just last week that the whole summer was sitting in front of him like a gallon of peppermint chocolate chip ice cream? He had a tablespoon in his hand and he was on his way down with the spoon to dig into all that cold minty goodness. Then at the last second, the spoon was cruelly jerked out of his hand by his parents before he even had one tiny bite. It was now official. This was going to be the worst summer ever.

Mrs. Field could read the misery on his face.

"Hey, Tuck Boy, I know you. I saw how much you cared for a dead rabbit in a jar. You're not going to let those crows die. You're going to do the right thing. They are very special creatures, you wait and see. I really think you are in for a pleasant surprise if you can stick with it," she said, messing up his hair with her hand.

As if, he thought sadly.

"Oh, as long as you gave me the pleasure of your company, I have this for you!" She slapped a stack of math activity sheets into his hands on top of the crow information. "Keep me updated on your birds!" she called out to him as he went out the front door.

10
A CRASH COURSE IN CROWS

THE RIDE BACK was mostly uphill and every time Tucker pushed down on one of the pedals of his bike it felt like he was trying to push a ton. His thoughts about his ruined summer seemed to make each pedal even harder. There was just no way out of his situation, absolutely none that he could think of. If it was so illegal to keep crows, maybe he'd get lucky and the police would come and take his bird. Maybe he'd even call the police on himself. He was feeling so frustrated that if he'd been at his house he'd have run down into his room, screamed into his pillow and given it a few good bites.

He pulled his bike into his driveway. Maddy was sitting there with the box.

"He's really cute and I really think he likes me. He doesn't seem to be as scared as he was. I think it's because I've been talking to him for almost the whole time you were gone." Tucker could easily believe that.

Mrs. McTeal came out the back door. "Well, what'd she say?"

Tucker handed her the papers that had the information about crows. Mrs. McTeal took the papers and quickly skimmed it with her eyes.

"Canned dog food, huh?" she said, looking at an area that Mrs. Field had highlighted. "Give me a couple of minutes to read this over and see what we have in the pantry." She went back in the house and came back out fifteen minutes later with a can of Bandit's dog food. "I'll bet this'll do," she said as she peeled of the lid of a fresh can. "Tuck, that article I read was pretty interesting. I'll bet you didn't know that a baby crow is called a simp!"

Tucker hadn't known and he didn't really care.

She reread some of the information and then said, "It says here you just scoop some food out with your finger and gently put it into the back of the simp's throat. Doesn't sound too hard." She handed Tucker the can. "Here you go. Let's see if he'll eat any. I'll bet it's been a while since he's had some food."

"Me? Can't you try it first?"

"I'll try it," said Maddy. That was all Tucker had to hear.

"Okay, give me the can." He curled his pointer finger into the shape of a hook. He dug his finger in and pulled a chunk of dog food out.

"Now you hafta stick your finger in his mouth!" squealed Maddy excitedly.

"I know, I know!"

Tucker was a bit nervous. He'd never done anything like this before. He figured it probably couldn't bite him very hard. But then again, you never know. After all, it was a wild animal.

"Remember, it has to end up in the back of his throat," his mom reminded him.

"I know, I know," he said again, a bit nervously. He took a deep breath and moved his finger toward the baby crow's head. He stuck it in front of his face. The bird just sat there with his mouth closed and blinked his eyes a couple of times.

"I don't think he wants anything right now," he said.

"Don't be silly. He just doesn't know what it is," his mom said. "You're going to have to try to get some inside his mouth."

Tucker felt himself starting to feel warm and his forehead felt sweaty. He tried again and attempted to push a bit of the food into the side of the crow's mouth, but the simp turned his head away.

"I've got an idea. The next time he opens his mouth to squawk, you're going to have to quickly get your finger in there."

Mrs. McTeal decided to help the situation by tilting the box to one side. The bird let out a squawk of objection as it began to slide to one side and Tucker was quick enough to get his finger in. The bird gave out another panicked squawk and tried to jerk his head away. But just enough of the dog food made it into the back of his throat and he swallowed. When that happened, the struggle to feed him was all over. His eyes grew wide and he threw his head back with his mouth wide open.

"Awww, awww!" he shrieked. Tucker's finger scooped up another chunk and he put it in his throat. "Gawba, gawba gawba!" he babbled as he ate it, sounding just like a turkey. The transformation was amazing and with every scoop he became more excited. He soon jumped to his feet and cawed, dancing with impatience and eagerness between mouthfuls.

"You're the smartest mommy in the world!" proclaimed Maddy.

Tucker continued to shovel in the food as fast as he could, trying to keep up with the bird's appetite. He had hardly ever felt so proud of himself in all his life. Soon his two younger sisters came out to investigate and giggled as they enjoyed the show.

"Just wait until Dad gets home from work! Boy, will he be surprised!" said Maddy.

Mrs. McTeal laughed. "Yes, he will be in for a surprise, that's for sure." No one was too worried about objections from Dad. He was always pretty easygoing and he had a real soft spot in his heart for animals. In fact, the reason they had Bandit was because Mr. McTeal found him in a recycling dumpster at work. He'd gone out to toss some paper into it and thought he saw a couple of white rats on the bottom of the container. It turned out that someone had dumped a liter of puppies in the dumpster and Ethan McTeal climbed into it to rescue them. He kept Bandit because he was the smallest and brought the others to an animal shelter.

Tucker was about three-fourths of the way through the can when the bird finally began to slow down. The squawking between mouthfuls grew quieter until finally it stopped. He put his finger near the bird's mouth, but it remained closed. The bird sat down in the towel and appeared to sigh. It closed and opened its eyes a few times and then fell asleep.

No doubt it was going to be a lot of work. But Tucker thought that perhaps it wasn't going to be as bad as he'd imagined after all.

He went inside and called his friends, who soon came back over to his house. They were all carrying their crows in boxes now and had various rags and towels stuffed in them to make a bird's nest. Mrs. McTeal was kind enough to pull out a couple more cans of dog food and Tucker was now eager to show them how to feed the crows. Even Maddy got into the act when Poodlehead and Benny and Josh let her take a turn at feeding their crows. Mrs. McTeal took some videos and snapped a few pictures.

"I'll need to post these so your Uncle Lowell and Aunt Diane can see this in Oklahoma."

They were just about done with the feeding when Benny's lips started trembling and he burst into tears.

"Benny, what's wrong?" asked Mrs. McTeal.

"My dad said I can't have the crow!" he sobbed. "He said that he hadn't ever let any of my brothers or sisters have a pet and that I can't have one either. My dad said it would cost money and be too much trouble!" He buried his face into his hands and wept. He turned and began to walk back toward home.

Mrs. McTeal ran over to him and put her arm around him. "I'm going to make you a deal, Benny. I've known you all your life and you've always been a kind and responsible boy. If you come over here to feed and take care of the crow every day, he can stay at our house. Do you promise? How does that sound?"

"Good," Benny said between sobs and wiping his eyes. "I promise."

"I can help feed your crow too, Benny!" Maddy chimed in.

Tucker was stunned. He'd never expected his mom to do something like this. He hadn't even been told yet that he was keeping his crow.

Mr. McTeal arrived home from work later that afternoon and while he was certainly a bit surprised by the day's events, he took it in stride as he did most things in life. In fact, he was so agreeable that he said he'd drop Tucker and Benny off at the library a little later so they could both do some crow research.

As they pulled up to the library, Tucker and Benny unbuckled and got out of the car.

"I'll be back in a couple hours to pick you up," Mr. McTeal said as the boys stepped out of the car and closed the doors.

"Thanks for the ride, Mr. McTeal," Benny said through the open car window.

"Yeah. Thanks, Dad."

"Oh, and boys…remember. No internet."

"But, Dad! That's impossible! How are we supposed to…?"

"Do it the old-fashioned way. Books. Magazines. Encyclopedias." Mr. McTeal smiled and drove off.

"Ahhhhhhh!" Tucker screamed into the air. "My parents are driving me crazy!" He and Benny made their way toward the library entrance.

"I'm not saying we should, but who would ever know if we used the library internet?" Benny asked, opening the library door.

"Are you kidding me? Knowing *my* parents, the librarians are spies and have already been tipped off about us," he joked.

"You're paranoid, dude!"

"Why…would you really want to chance it?"

"I don't know. I'm just sayin'. It sure would be a lot easier."

But before they had a chance to take the idea any further, a plump middle-aged woman with a pleasant smile on her face walked up to them.

"Hello, boys, can I help you with something?"

"Uh, yeah," Tucker answered. "We need to look up information about crows."

"Ah, yes, crows! I was right; you are the two boys. One of your mothers called a little while ago and told me you'd be coming and what you were looking for. I already have a nice pile of books and magazines for you to get started!"

Tucker and Benny looked at each other in stunned disbelief.

The boys grabbed the stacks of material and found an isolated corner of the library. As they paged through the books and magazines, one thing that kept jumping out at both of them was the high level of intelligence that the birds possessed. It was a theme that repeated itself in every book and every article.

"Tuck, look at this," Benny said, pushing his magazine over to Tucker and pointing excitedly at a paragraph. "It says here that crows are one of the most intelligent animals on the planet. They're smarter than dogs. They think they may even be smarter than chimps! This is too cool!"

"I know, I've been coming across the same thing. I thought a bird was pretty much a bird. I mean, I knew crows were bigger than other birds. I knew they didn't sing like other birds. But that was about it."

"Look down at what the next paragraph says. It says that when a crow comes upon a new situation, they can figure out a solution to it and make a tool to solve it. It says no other animal—not dogs, dolphins or even chimps—can do that. Tucker, this is too cool!"

"Benny, you said that already."

"I know, but I'm pumped! I've never had a pet before and now I get the smartest animal on the planet!"

"Keep it quiet back there please," came the voice of the woman who'd helped them earlier.

Benny looked over at Tucker. Tucker crossed his eyes, made a nasty, scrunched-up face and whispered in an old woman's voice, "Keep it quiet back there please," giving his head a wobble for effect. Benny put his hand over his mouth and tried to smother his laugh. Seeing this, Tucker put his hands on his hips and began to open and close his mouth in an exaggerated way with no words coming out as he gave Benny an angry lecture. Benny grabbed his mouth tighter, trying to hold back the laughter. Tucker shot out his hand and started shaking his finger in Benny's face. That was all Benny could take. His laughter burst though his fingers and into the room. Tucker quickly grabbed his book and pretended to read it.

"If you boys can't behave yourself back here, I'll have to ask you to come up and sit at the front table where I can keep an eye on you," said the librarian as she walked toward them.

"I'm sorry, ma'am. I told you to stop playing around, Benny," Tucker said in his most serious voice. "I'll try to get him to stop." Benny had his elbows on the table and face in his hands as his body shook with uncontrollable laughter.

"See that you do."

Mr. McTeal returned as he had promised a while later and the boys not only left the library with books, but with a new appreciation for their crows.

As he studied about crows more at home, Tucker discovered that crow babies won't normally poop in their nests. In the wild, they back their rear ends out over the nest and then do their business. Nothing ends up inside the nest. That made sense to Tucker. Simps wouldn't be able to stay too long in a nest if they were filling it with their own waste. After reading this and thinking about the box that held his crow, he came up with an idea. He explained his plan to his dad who brought him out to the garage and they got to work.

Tucker found two metal trays and placed the two simps' boxes into each tray. They then cut off one end of the cardboard boxes so that the birds could back out and poop into the tray. Tucker had doubts on whether this was going to work; it didn't look like a typical bird's nest. But he hadn't needed to worry. Because as soon as their new nests were ready to go, despite no one showing or guiding them on what to do, both crows went right ahead and did their business as if they'd been doing it that way all their lives. It was a pretty incredible sight. Tucker never dreamed he could be so impressed by watching a bird poop. Maybe crows really were as smart as the books said.

Since it appeared that he was going to be saddled with the responsibility of a crow all summer, Tucker began to think that it may as well have a name. He'd never liked your average run-of-the-mill names for animals and he'd never been too impressed by the common everyday names people had for their pets like Spike, Muffin, or Buddy. Boring! He liked names that could make people smile or names that were unique. For example, he had wanted to name the family dog Spam, because no one was exactly sure where he came from or what he was. But the family voted for Bandit. Bandit was not a horrible choice, but not as good as Spam, he thought.

Later that evening, he brought his bird down into his basement bedroom with him. Maddy had volunteered to take care of the other simp in her room. Tucker studied the plump and almost naked bird as it sat in the box on the edge of his bed.

"You're so young you're barely out of the egg," he said out loud to the bird. "In fact, you're not much more than an egg yourself." The bird looked up at the sound of the boy's voice, blinking his enormous crow eyes.

"Egg," he chuckled. "That's a great name! From now on, you're Egg."

That night went well. Only once did he have to get up and give Egg something to eat and even then he didn't seem real hungry, eating only about one quarter of the amount he'd normally eat. Tucker thought he seemed more lonesome than hungry and just wanted some comfort. Benny's crow didn't eat at all.

They'd kept Bandit away from the birds during the first day they'd brought the crows home, but thought it would be wise to try to introduce them to him now. Bandit was a gentle dog who was also a very curious one. Maddy held him as he sniffed the two boxes and looked inside. He whimpered a little and tried to lick Egg, but Maddy pulled him back.

"It's too soon for kisses!" she said. It was clear that Bandit was not going to be a problem.

Benny was the first one of the boys to stop over the next morning. He hadn't slept well that night because he'd been thinking about his new pet. They took the birds outside and fed them. The crows behaved just like the day before, cawing and opening their mouths wide, swallowing the dog food as fast as the boys could shovel it in. Tucker's mom came out to watch.

"Here," Benny said, handing Mrs. McTeal a ten-dollar bill.

"Why…why are you giving me this?"

"It's to pay for the dog food. I have money."

"Benny, you don't have to do that. We get it wholesale for practically nothing. We know someone who gives us a break on it because we don't care if the cans are bent or damaged." She tried to hand it back, but Benny refused.

"It's my crow and I want to pay for him." Mrs. McTeal could see in his eyes that it was important to him.

"Okay, Benny. It's a deal," she said, putting the money in her pocket. She smiled at him and went back in the house.

"So, did you name him yet?" Tucker asked. There was no way of knowing whether the birds were male or female, but all the boys just assumed their crows were male.

"Yep," Benny said with a smile. "Did you name yours?"

"Uh huh," he said, also smiling. "You go first."

"I named him Moe," Benny said.

"Why Moe? Where does that come from?"

"You know, Moe from The Three Stooges. When my dad first came to this country, he didn't speak any English, so he didn't understand very many things. Well, one day he was watching TV and he saw The Three Stooges. He didn't have to understand much of what they were saying to be able to know what was going on, so he started watching them all the time."

"Wow, Benny, your dad would have been the last guy I'd have ever thought would be a Stooges fan. Does he actually laugh out loud at them?"

"No. But you can kind of see in his eyes that he is laughing inside. Anyway, I think he owns every Three Stooges video out there, so I grew up watching them all the time. My dad liked Moe the best because he's always the boss."

"That's pretty cool. Really cool, actually."

"So what'd you name yours?"

"Egg."

"What?"

"Egg. You know...like an egg."

"Okay..." Benny said, smiling and raising one eyebrow.

"What? What's the problem with that?"

"That's the stupidest name I ever heard in my life! But you know what? It's so stupid that it's way cool!" he said. They both started laughing so hard that tears came to their eyes.

A little later, the other boys came over with their crows. Poodlehead held his box a bit awkwardly because his head was still hunched over on the side of his neck.

"Wow, Poodles, it looks like your neck still doesn't feel any better."

"Nah, my dad said it's going to take a while. It's too bad this didn't happen near Halloween. I could've gone as the Hunchback of Notre Dame!" The funny thing about it was that he wasn't joking. One thing about Poodlehead is that he never seemed to take himself too seriously.

Josh's parents didn't mind him having the crow at all. Poodlehead's dad wasn't crazy about the idea, but since the only other alternative was letting Evil Caesar eat him, he couldn't say no. Aside from that, Poodlehead's dad was still a bit shook up about Scotty's ride in the Kooky Kastle and Poodlehead was milking it for all its worth. Josh had named his crow Midnight, but Poodlehead hadn't made up his mind on what to name his crow yet.

"I kind of like Batman, but Batman can't really fly like a bird; he glides." Poodlehead loved superheroes.

"You are going to name your crow Batman?" Josh asked with a sour look on his face.

"No. I was just thinking what if I did."

"That's pretty bad, Poodles," Tucker added. "Admit it, you were serious. That kind of doesn't even make sense."

"Oh, and Egg makes sense?"

"More than naming a crow Batman."

"Hey, whatever happened to Crandal? He never showed yesterday," Benny said. "We should stop over and show him what we found."

"It's probably better that he wasn't there since there are only four crows," said Josh.

No one said anything, but they all agreed. Benny thought about it for a moment and realized that he would have been the one left out because his dad didn't allow pets. It was only through the kindness of Mrs. McTeal that he had his.

They made their way over to Crandal's house. It was close to eleven o'clock when they knocked on the door.

They knocked and knocked, but no one answered. Finally, just as they turned to leave, Crandal came to the door.

"What time is it?" he asked, looking through the screen door He squinted his eyes at the sunlight. He was wearing a t-shirt and pajama bottoms.

"Almost eleven."

"What have you guys got in the boxes?" He opened the door and went outside.

"We found some crows in Northwood Park yesterday. You should have been there; Evil Caesar killed their mother and he almost killed them, too!" Benny said. "We saved their lives!"

Crandal sat down on the step and rubbed his eyes.

"Hey, where were you yesterday?" Josh asked. "You said you were coming down there and you never showed. You could have got yourself a crow, too."

Crandal yawned, sighed, and scratched his head. He was still half-asleep.

"Yesterday? Oh yeah. I had planned to come down. I don't know. I got distracted or something." He looked over at Poodlehead's box. "What do you want those things for anyway? All they're going to do is steal all your time. You guys are going to be a bunch of babysitters." He smiled. "I wish you guys could have seen what I did in the game yesterday. Greatest move ever. I actually saved it in a file so you guys can see the replay when you can play video games again. You are not going to believe it."

"Crandal, you wanna know what we named our birds?" Josh asked, trying to change the subject. "Egg,

Midnight, and Moe," he said while he pointed at the boxes. "Poodlehead hasn't decided on his name yet."

Crandal looked over at Poodlehead's crow and smirked. "How about you name him Lou?"

"Lou?" asked Poodlehead.

"Yeah, Lou. His last name would be Sirr. Lou Sirr. He'd be a perfect match for you, Poodlehead!"

"Knock it off, Crandal," Poodlehead said. He could tell by Crandal's tone where he was going with this.

"What a minute. How about Buttmuncher!" he said as he started laughing. "I'll bet he'll be real good at that. Wait, here's a good one! How about…"

"How about you just shut up, Grimy," Josh said. "Why do you always have to make fun of people? What makes you think you're better than everybody else?"

Maybe it was because he'd just woken up. Maybe he felt safe sitting on his back step close to his back door. Or maybe it was because he was in one of his bad moods. But to everyone's surprise, Crandal answered, "How about you shut up, four eyes. And why don't you go and buy some real clothes for a change? You look like you found your shirt and pants on the side of the highway. You look like a hillbilly fool."

"Uh, oh," said Benny.

Josh put his box down.

"What'd you say, Grimy Beans?" Josh said, staring at him intensely.

Crandal wouldn't look Josh in the eyes, so he looked at the ground. He knew he had better be careful, even if he was sitting on his own back steps. He stood up, turned around, and opened the door and went inside his house.

"Get out of my yard, losers," he said through the screen door.

11
EGG

"YOU'RE PRETTY BRAVE standing behind that door, Grimy. Why don't you come out here?"

"You heard me, Josh. I said get out of my yard. You too, Poodlehead. Go babysit your winged rats. Tucker and Benny, you can stay if you want."

Josh was mad. So mad that he grabbed the handle and tried to pull the door open. But Crandal had wisely locked the screen door.

"Crandal, who's at the door?" came a voice from inside the house. It was Crandal's mom.

Crandal turned and shouted, "No one, Ma. It's just some of the guys. They were just leaving." Crandal turned and looked out the screen door.

"See ya, Hillbilly," he said, looking at Josh and closing the inside door.

Tucker wondered what had set Crandal off. He'd always been a bit moody and self-centered, but he'd never gone after Josh that way.

"He better stay hiding with his mom in his house. Next time I see him, I'll squeeze his head so hard it'll pop like a big zit."

"I'd like to see that, Josh. Just make sure I'm there when you do it. Buttmuncher! He called my crow Buttmuncher! He's the buttmuncher, not my crow."

"Hey, guys. You've seen Crandal act like a jerk before. By tomorrow he'll act like nothing happened. Don't make a bigger deal out of it than it is."

"Whose side are you on, Tucker? He made fun of my clothes and called me a hillbilly. Plus, he's always making fun of Poodlehead or someone else."

"I'm just saying Crandal is Crandal. He says stuff to everybody. I'm not saying he was right. That's just the way he is."

"Yeah, Tuck's right," said Benny. "He says stuff to me all the time, but I just ignore it."

"I tell you one thing. He better knock that hillbilly stuff off."

"And that buttmunching stuff," added Poodlehead.

"Knowing Crandal, he probably won't even remember he said those things in a couple days. He makes up so many names he can't keep track of it all."

Tucker figured it would all blow over pretty quickly. This wasn't the first time Crandal had done something like this and he was sure it wouldn't be the last. Josh was mad now, but he wasn't one to hold a grudge, especially against a friend. And Poodlehead could never stay angry with anyone. He'd call Crandal later and try to straighten things out.

The next two weeks were very busy. Egg slept in his box at the side of Tucker's bed. Every morning pretty much followed the same routine. Egg would sit quietly in his "nest" and intensely watch every little movement Tucker made. As soon as Tucker would open his eyes or give any other indication that he was awake, Egg would jump to his feet and start squawking, which Tucker knew meant, "Feed me! Feed me!" His cawing would quickly grow frantic if Tucker left the room to get his food in the morning; he didn't like to be kept waiting for breakfast. So Tucker learned to keep a can of the dog food near his bed so he could just roll over and start feeding Egg. The dog food had to be hidden because if Egg caught a glimpse of it, that too set off his cries for food. After Egg was done eating, Tucker would pull the bird up next to him. Egg would snuggle up close, give a sigh and then drift back to sleep as he drew warmth from the boy's body. Tucker would gently place Egg back in his nest and then go get breakfast for himself.

Benny more than held up his share of the load and was always at the McTeal's door first thing in the morning. If Maddy hadn't gotten up yet to feed Moe, he'd make sure Moe was fed his breakfast. Benny and Tucker also had the daily job of taking out the metal trays that the bird boxes sat in and spraying them clean with the garden house. The four boys traveled almost everywhere with their birds and they all took their jobs very seriously. Poodlehead eventually decided to name his crow Robin.

He explained to Tucker that once he realized that he couldn't name his crow Batman, he figured naming him after Batman's partner was the next best choice. He still got to use a superhero name and it also had a weird double meaning since it was another type of bird. All agreed that it was a better choice than Batman. Dr. Zeimer also fitted him with a nice front tooth (which Poodlehead could still pop out when the mood struck him) and his stiff neck was now completely healed. After talking with Crandal and Josh, Tucker helped patch things up between the two boys. Tucker talked Crandal into promising never to call Josh "hillbilly" again or make fun of his clothes. In turn, Josh promised not to pop Crandal's head like a pimple with his famous headlock. Poodlehead never mentioned the incident again, but oddly enough started using the word "buttmuncher" so much that everyone got sick of it and told him to stop using it so much. But even after the incident blew over, things weren't the same. They started seeing less and less of Crandal and Tucker wasn't sure why. Crandal always seemed to have an excuse not to join them.

After two weeks, the crows were very aware of who their owners were. If they were placed down in the grass, they would venture out to investigate their new world, but then eventually hop back toward the one who had been taking care of them. While Moe had made a connection to Benny, he also had a fondness for Maddy since she spent time a lot of time with him, too. Moe would sometimes hop to her even when Benny was around which made

Maddy proud because she knew that it showed that she had been taking good care of him.

"He thinks I'm his mommy!" she would proudly proclaim.

Some pet owners might have felt threatened by this, but Benny would just laugh. He was so happy to just have a crow that it never occurred to him to be jealous.

Egg's adult feathers came in and he spent much of his time hopping and fluttering about. Tucker would watch him in the backyard. He would run, hop, and flutter. Run, hop, and flutter. Tucker knew that he was practicing for the day when he would be able to take flight. The box that was used to carry Egg around in was now only used for naps and bedtime. Egg had also become aware that with a hop and a flutter he could jump out of the box anyway.

Everywhere Tucker went, Egg went too and he'd be firmly attached to Tucker's arm or shoulder. The half-hour feedings began to stretch out to once an hour and then longer. The two spent so much time together that it soon seemed that Egg had always been there and Tucker couldn't imagine his life without him. Tucker's relationship with Egg was evolving from one of caretaker to one of friend. Under the warm Minnesota summer sun he'd stretch out in the grass and Egg would soon be on top of him, hopping his way up to his face. Egg would poke and pull at his nose and lips and then hop onto his face so that he could play with and pull at his hair. When Tucker would talk to him, Egg would cluck back and cock his head sideways, appearing as if he understood what Tucker was saying. Tucker would tire of having his hair yanked and pulled and move to a sitting position. Egg would always take that opportunity to make his way to the very top of Tucker's head and then stand there tall and proud.

"I get the funny feeling that this is your way of showing me who's the boss!" Tucker would then reach up and pull him down from his perch and stroke Egg's head. Egg would close his eyes and lean into it, nuzzling his head against Tucker's palm

Tucker smiled when he thought back to just a few weeks before when he had been so completely sure that it was going to be the worst summer of his life. Since the day he'd been banned from video games, he and his friends had no choice but to return to many of the activities that they used to enjoy, like hiking into Cowern Woods, playing baseball and basketball at the park, or skateboarding down the steep hill by Tucker's house. They started going swimming again at the public swimming pool and riding their bikes to go swimming or fishing at Silver Lake. Occasionally, Tucker could even talk Crandal into joining them. But even when he did show up for something, his mind always seemed to be somewhere else and he wouldn't stay long.

One day, Tucker had been in the backyard with Egg riding on his shoulder when Egg suddenly leaped off and fluttered about fifteen feet through the air and landed on the picnic table.

"Wow, Egg! Way to go!" Tucker hollered.

"Maddy! Mom! You gotta get out here and see what Egg can do!" he shouted as he ran into the house. Maddy dashed outside, as did Mrs. McTeal and the younger girls.

They didn't have to wait long because Egg fluttered right back onto Tucker's arm.

"He can fly! I can't believe it!" Maddy shouted, "Good job, Egg, we knew you could do it!" Tucker made quick calls to the rest of his friends and they were soon at his house with their crows.

"Excell-aun-tay, grome-ay-graun-tay!" exclaimed Poodlehead. "Have him do it again. I want Robin to see him do it!"

Egg seemed more than willing and gave off the impression that he was just as excited to show off his newfound skill as everyone was to watch it. He soon was flapping his way to the swing set, then to the clothesline pole, then to the shed, and finally up to the gutter on the roof. His rate of learning and the distance he could fly seemed to be increasing with every attempt.

"Snap! Your crow is a genius!" Josh proclaimed. Tucker just smiled and nodded. He felt as proud as if he had learned to fly himself.

"C'mon down now Egg, c'mon down!" Tucker shouted to Egg who sat high above him on the gutter. Egg just stared at him. Tucker held out his arm.

"C'mon boy, come back down to me," he called again.

Egg cocked his head sideways and then began looking around, appearing like he hadn't heard a word.

"Maybe he's scared of heights," Maddy offered.

This went on for a few minutes until Tucker tired of it and got out the ladder. Egg watched him climb to the top and hold out his arm. Egg looked at the arm and then leaped out into the air and flew over to the apple tree.

"Uh oh. Maybe I don't want Robin to fly so badly now," Poodlehead said.

"Yeah, me too," said Benny.

Tucker climbed down the ladder and went over to the tree and started to climb toward Egg. But as he neared him, Egg flew right back to the gutter. Tucker's heart sank a bit. After all, they'd grown pretty close the last few weeks and now that Egg had learned to fly he seemed to want to have nothing to do with him. Tucker climbed down the tree and stared up at Egg perched on the gutter. He wasn't about to climb the ladder again just to watch him fly away.

Suddenly Maddy had an idea. She ran into the house and came out with a can of dog food and handed it to Tucker. He immediately knew what she was thinking and he held up the can and called out, "Egg!"

As soon as Egg's blue-grey eyes caught a glimpse of the can, he was off the roof and on Tucker's arm, cawing loudly and holding his mouth wide open.

"Not so independent after all, eh Egg?" he said. "Good job, Maddy." Maddy beamed.

It was Egg's first step toward becoming more independent and it wouldn't be his last. Within just a day or two, the other birds were flying, too. Within a few days, another milestone occurred. Egg sat perched on the house gutter in the backyard—which was becoming one of his favorite spots to sit and observe things—when Tucker called him in for the night.

"Egg, time to come in, I'm going to bed."

Egg looked at him and then looked the other way.

"Hey, don't play around, it's starting to get dark. Let's go!"

Egg just stared back, acting like he had no idea what that boy was talking about. Tucker sighed, went into the house and brought out the ever-dependable can of dog food. This never failed. Egg looked at the dog food for a moment, decided it held no interest for him at the moment and then turned his head to watch some sparrows flying in the distance.

"If you don't come down right now, I'll leave you out here!" he threatened.

Tucker then went inside the house and shut the door. He paced in the kitchen for about five minutes, thinking that Egg just needed some time to realize that it was time to come in for the night. Tucker went back out to try to coax him inside one more time, but to his surprise and dismay, Egg was gone. He called out his name and walked around the yard for a good ten minutes, but it was growing darker and with Egg's dark black coloring he was unable to see him anywhere. He finally had to give up and go to bed, wondering if he'd ever see his crow again.

He spent a restless night worrying about Egg's fate. Would an owl get him? What about a cat? He shuddered when the thought of Evil Caesar crossed his mind. Earlier that evening, Maddy had gotten Moe to come in for the night very easily. Why did Egg always have to be so stubborn and independent? He'd be so much safer in the basement than out in the deep dark night. Egg had no idea of the dangers that lurked out there.

When morning finally arrived, Tucker was up as soon as the first rays of light began to spread across the dark sky. While he was anxious to go out and search for Egg, he was also afraid to face what might have happened to him. The image of the torn body of Egg's mother was still very fresh in his mind. Did Egg meet that same fate? Would he find his body on the ground somewhere, shredded to pieces by an owl, a dog, or a cat?

He made his way out the back door and looked over at the gutter on the house. No Egg. His eyes scanned some of his other favorite perches: the top of the shed, the clothesline pole, the apple tree. No Egg.

What if Egg had decided to fly away and never returned? Was he really capable of living on his own already? Tucker didn't think so. If Egg had flown off for good, then Tucker would never know what became of him.

Finally, he held up the dog food can and hollered out, "Egg!"

A sudden streak of black flew out of the neighbor's large oak tree and made its way toward him. A great wave of relief came over Tucker. He landed on Tucker's arm, cawing and opening his mouth wide enough to show every detail of the inside of his bright red mouth. He stroked Egg's head and told him how worried he'd been about him that night. He then fed him until he stopped cawing.

From that night on, Egg never spent another night indoors and eventually Tucker had to get used to the idea that Egg wasn't the same needy creature from just a few weeks back. He was stunned by how fast it had all happened and he wished he could somehow slow time down.

Within a week or so, the other crows decided that they preferred staying outdoors at night, too. This wasn't all bad, because now Benny could bring Moe home at night and he'd roost in a nearby group of trees near Benny's house. Mrs. McTeal would let him bring a can of dog food home at night and much like Egg, Moe would come streaking out of the trees the first thing in the morning when Benny came out the door to give him his breakfast. Maddy was a bit disappointed at first when Moe was no longer staying overnight with her, but she understood it was all quite normal since she had already watched Egg become independent.

As the summer wore, Tucker was surprised by how many adults would walk up to him to tell about a fond memory they had of a specific crow they'd known as a child. It might have been a neighbor's pet crow or a wild crow that had decided it enjoyed interacting with humans. Tucker began to wonder how these intelligent and unusual birds could have existed all around him for all these years without him noticing them. Even with all his research, he realized how little he really knew about crows; he seemed to learn something new about Egg everyday.

Since the world began to seem like such a friendlier place since Egg came into his life, Tucker fantasized about what would happen if he was walking down the street and Monique Dubois just happened to be strolling by. She'd have to stop and tell him how cute and smart she thought Egg was. He'd let it slip how he'd taken on Evil Caesar and saved Egg's life. Then he'd start rattling off all the amazing facts that he now knew about crows, impressing her not only with his bravery but with his knowledge about these clever birds. Her big brown eyes would open wide with amazement. He could almost hear her giggling at his witty comments.

This is going to be the worst summer ever! he recalled thinking when he was at Mrs. Field's house. *Correction*, he thought, *this is going to be the best summer ever!*

12
DON'T TELL YOUR MOTHER I'M DOWN HERE

"YOU KNOW WHAT we have to do this summer? We have to sleep out in the field," Poodlehead suddenly said out of nowhere as he cast his fishing line into Silver Lake.

They'd all ridden their bikes the two miles to the lake with their fishing poles and bait and were fishing from the shore on the north side of the lake at a place people called Joy Park. They'd made sure that Maddy and some of her friends had kept the crows distracted with food when they took off for their little trip because there would have been a good chance that at least one or maybe all of them would have tried to follow along. While the boys never minded the crows tagging along when they were around the neighborhood, they didn't want them to get lost if they followed them for that distance to an unfamiliar area.

"Got another one," said Josh. There was the sound of his line being reeled in and the splash of water as the fish fought being brought to shore.

"Snap! Another bullhead," he said as he lifted it out of the water. "You want him, Tucker?"

"Sure, just put him on my stringer." No one but Tucker kept bullheads.

"I wish I could keep these. But I ain't cleaning bull-head," said Josh. Bullhead were difficult to clean since they had skin instead of scales and the others didn't think they were worth the trouble. They also had what the boys called stingers near the front of their faces that left a painful welt on your hand if you accidentally touched it.

Plop went the bobber as Tucker's line hit the water. It was soon followed with a *clickety, clickety* as he reeled in his fish. *Plop, clickety, clickety. Plop, clickety, clickety.*

"Man alive, maybe I should start my own fishing show!" he bragged as he reeled in another fish. Tucker was having a good day: five bullheads, one smallmouth bass, and nine sunfish. He now had a total of fifteen fish on his stringer and he felt that had made the trip worthwhile. The others had been having about the same luck, but they had fewer fish to show for it since they didn't keep bullheads and many of the sunfish were not keepers.

"Sleeping out in the field, huh? That's a great idea!" Benny said. "We'll get a fire going and cook hotdogs and marshmallows. We can make s'mores!"

"Let's do it tonight!" Josh said. "Summer is going to be gone and we'll be back in school before we know it."

Tucker was the only one who hadn't said anything. Even though some time had passed after his disastrous sleepover, he wasn't sure how his parents would feel about him camping out in the field. He went back and forth in his head about whether he should even ask. He finally decided that he might as well. The worst thing they could say was no and give him a lecture about what happened at his party.

"Yeah," he finally said, "it sounds like a good idea."

The feeding frenzy began to slow down and then abruptly stopped. Tucker walked about a dozen yards to his left and then made his way over to an area where an old log sat in some shallow water and cast his line there. He stared at his bobber, but the only ripple around it came when he wiggled his pole a bit to try to move his line away from the log. After fishing for another half hour and getting skunked, the boys decided to pack it in. Tucker pulled the stake out of the ground and started to pull his stringer full of fish out of the water. He couldn't wait to get them cleaned. Maybe his mom might even fry them up for supper tonight. There was hardly anything that tasted as good as fish caught from a lake and eaten the same day. Who knows, maybe a plate full of delicious fresh fish for dinner might even soften his parents up when he asked them if he could go camping in the field tonight.

"What in the world…" he said as he pulled the stringer from the water. All his fish were gone. Well, almost gone. There were a few fish heads left hanging morbidly on the stringer.

"Stupid, stupid snapping turtles!" said Josh. "It's been so long since we've gone fishing here, I forgot all about them. We should have been tossing them into a bucket of water."

The other boys quickly pulled in their stringers and, sure enough, all that were left on their stringers were a few fish heads.

"Well, we sure served them up nice and easy for those snappers. They must have thought they were at a restaurant today," Benny said.

"Maybe next time we come, we should fish for snapping turtles," Tucker said, only half-joking. "I wonder if turtle soup is any good."

They loaded up their things and headed back toward home. Despite their bad luck, they had enjoyed another beautiful day in a string of beautiful Minnesota summer days.

As they started to make their way toward home, Tucker drank in the beauty of Silver Lake and took deep breaths of all the wonderful smells of a summer day by a lake.

"You know what I was thinking?" Poodlehead asked.

"What?" said Tucker.

"That this beats any video game we ever played."

"You think the weirdest things, Poodles," Tucker said, but deep down, he felt that way, too.

To Tucker's surprise, his parents didn't seem to mind at all if he camped out. In fact, they seemed to think it wasn't a bad idea. Sometimes he wondered if he'd ever figure them out.

"I used to camp out a lot with my friends when I was growing up," his dad said. "Those are some of the best memories I have of my childhood."

Tucker decided to give Crandal a call and get him to join them.

"Hey, Crandal! What are you doing tonight?"

"I'm playing *Death Valley Death Virus,* man! It's awesome! I'm on the verge of pretty much taking over a whole town of mutant cowboys. I'm part of a posse of vigilantes that are trying to save their town. Whoda thought I could get into a western game, but this really rocks! Can you beg your parents to come over and play just for tonight? With you riding by my side, we'd dominate!"

It had been a long time since Tucker had played a video game and the thought of playing even *Death Valley Death Virus* sounded exciting.

"Crandal, you know I'd love to play. But the reason I was calling was that we're all camping out in the field tonight, just like we used to. Me, Benny, Josh, and Poodlehead. We're going to have a fire and everything. You can save where you are on the game and play it tomorrow."

There was a pause, as if Crandal was thinking it over.

"Tuck, it sounds tempting. But I am so unbelievably close to taking over the cowboy town. I think if I went with you guys I'd be thinking about the game the whole time anyway."

"Are you sure? Summer doesn't last forever around here, you know."

"Ehhh, there's plenty of summer left. Don't worry, I'll get around to camping out with you jokers, or maybe we'll do something else. It's just not a good time."

After calling the other three boys and finding out that they had permission also, he started to pack. A sleeping bag, granola and chocolate bars, graham crackers, marshmallows, a half a pack of hot dogs and buns, mustard and ketchup packets, beef jerky, a flashlight, his dad's hatchet (for chopping up branches for firewood), and a jug of water. He got a large trash bag and put them all inside. Mr. McTeal said he'd come out later to check out their camp and make sure that the fire pit that they dug had been set up properly.

"Remember, you can set it up, but no fire until I get out there," he warned.

With Egg on his shoulder, Tucker met the others (who also had brought their crows) at the park about an hour before dark and they made their way out to the field. All of them had been in scouting so they knew what they needed to do to set up camp. Benny had brought a small shovel to clear out a place to make a fire. The first thing they did was find a nice flat area where Benny and Poodlehead could put up their tents. A lump in the ground meant a long uncomfortable night in a sleeping bag. As they set up the tents, Tucker and Josh began walking toward Cowern Woods, which was only about a couple hundred feet east of them, in search of branches and old logs. Tucker had his trusty hatchet in hand and Egg and Midnight were with them. The crows played and pulled at the hair of each boy and interacted with each other with squawks and gargling noises.

Because of the storm that came through in June, they were able to find a lot of large dead branches on the ground. Tucker began hacking away at the branches with the hatchet and Josh found a few nice-sized old logs that looked like they'd been sitting on the forest floor for years. The crows flew up to a nearby tree, watching the activity and biting at each other with their beaks.

Tucker and Josh returned to camp with arms full of wood. Egg and Midnight had stayed in the tree, but flew from them and again landed on Tucker and Josh's shoulders as the boys got closer to the camp. Benny and Poodlehead already had their tents up and Benny was digging out an area for the fire. They surrounded the pit with large rocks and stones. It was a pit that any Boy Scout would be proud of. The crows had gathered together on the ground and, aside from wrestling around with each other, appeared to be looking for bugs and insects in the field. After a while, Egg appeared bored with it all and suddenly flew toward the park. A few seconds later, the others followed.

"Oh well," said Poodlehead. "They know where we are and they know how to get home, too, if they want." His attention turned to Benny as he watched him set up the wood for the fire. "Benny, you've always been able to get a good fire going."

"You have to do this just right," Benny answered as he meticulously placed small twigs over a layer of shredded birch bark. "You start small, that's the secret. I slowly go to bigger and bigger sticks. It takes longer, but it pays off in the end. If you try to start out with anything bigger, it never works."

As the light began to slowly fade, they could see a figure making its way through the park toward them. As it came closer, they could see that it was Mr. McTeal.

Mr. McTeal looked at the pit and then the rocks that the boys had piled around it.

"Wow, looks like you boys did an expert job with setting up your camp. It appears you guys were paying attention when you were in scouting." Benny had a big smile on his face, since he was the one who'd done most of the work.

"Okay, who gets to start the fire?"

They all agreed that should be Benny.

"Think you can be in the one match club?" asked Mr. McTeal.

Benny nodded and Mr. McTeal gave him a wooden match from his top pocket.

"Now just strike the match across the whiskers on your face like a real cowboy to get it going," Mr. McTeal kidded.

Benny laughed. He scraped the match over a rock and a bright yellow flame burst out from it. He touched it to the birch bark and it burst into a small flame. In a minute, the twigs were burning and the fire was spreading to the larger sticks.

"Looks like you're in the one match club," Poodle-head said.

The sun was almost gone and soon the fire had grown to a respectable size. Sticks were gathered and soon hot-dogs and marshmallows were being roasted, toasted and devoured.

"Hey, where's your old pal Crandal? Doesn't he usually hang out with you guys?" Mr. McTeal asked.

"I called and invited him, but he said he was busy with something," Tucker said. He really hadn't expected that Crandal would come, but he was glad he tried.

As they finished eating, as the fire snapped and popped, the boys started telling spooky stories. Benny told one about Evil Caesar that he'd heard from an older brother, about how he had attacked kids sleeping in this very same field. Tucker shuddered and tried to look for any movement in the dark woods near them. Benny's story was a bit too real for him. Poodlehead ended with his best scary story called "The Window Watcher." The story was about a man who kept calling up some girls that were all alone in their house and telling them that he was the "Window Watcher." As soon as the man would say those words, the terrified girls would immediately hang up on him. It turned out that the caller was in fact just a Swedish janitor. When he showed up at their door, he exclaimed in a thick Swedish accent, "I'm the window watsher and I've come to watsh your windows!" It was then that the girls realized he hadn't come to *watch* windows, he had come to *wash* them.

"Booo!" said Josh. "Not even scary."

"Hey, I tried," Poodlehead said.

"Tell us one of your scary stories, Dad," said Tucker.

"Are you guys sure you can handle one being out here all alone in the dark?"

"Sure!"

"No problem!" they answered.

"Okay then. Here we go," he said, rubbing his hands together, leaning toward the fire and lowering his voice.

"One day, little Leroy was playing outside in the bright sunshine. He was in his sandbox with his trucks and cars, having a good old time. It wasn't long before his mother called out the back door.

"She called out, 'Leroy! I need you to come in the house and help me with something!'

"'Aw mom, do I have to?' he answered.

"'Yes, and don't be giving me any lip!'" Mr. McTeal said in a woman's voice and shaking his finger in the air.

The boys quietly chuckled.

"'I need you to run down the basement and get me some potatoes for supper.' Leroy froze in his tracks! The basement? Did she say the basement? Leroy was deathly afraid to go down there. You see, his basement wasn't the kind of nice finished basements you all have in your houses. His basement was more like an old cellar, with big rocks mortared together for walls and only a couple of light bulbs with a string attached to them. Even with the lights turned on, it was dark and shadowy. The basement had a damp, musty smell to it and there were huge spider webs everywhere."

The boys were focused on the story now and they all stared intently at Mr. McTeal's glowing face.

"'Take this potato sack and bring me up about seven potatoes. Now hurry up about it!' Leroy knew it would do no good to argue. He opened the old creaky door to the basement and started going down the old creaky stairs. There was no light bulb until he reached the bottom of the stairs, so he went down in total darkness. Finally, he reached the basement floor and his hand reached out into the darkness to find the string so that he could pull it and turn on the light. His hand searched and searched," said Mr. McTeal as his own hand moved back and forth near the fire, "and his hand ended up in some cobwebs and he felt a spider run up his arm."

Josh shuddered. "I hate spiders."

"Finally, he felt it," Mr. McTeal said as he clenched his own fist and yanked it downward. "He pulled the string and while it gave him some light, it was still pretty dark down there. He went to the back room and again had to feel for a string. This time he found it right away. He went into the corner bin where the potatoes were stored and began filling his sack. One potato... Two potatoes... What was that?"

Mr. McTeal turned to look dramatically behind him. The boys' eyes searched into the darkness, thinking perhaps that somehow Mr. McTeal's story was becoming real.

"But there was nothing there. Six potatoes. Seven potatoes. Done! Leroy breathed a sigh of relief as he grabbed his sack and got to his feet. He reached up and turned off the light and started to hurry as fast as he could toward the basement steps.

"But wait! What was that? Did he hear footsteps behind him? He turned and looked into the darkness, but could see nothing. He began to walk again toward the light when he was sure he heard the footsteps again. He looked back again. There was just enough light now for him to see that there was nothing behind him. He breathed another sigh of relief and walked toward the hanging string that was attached to the light bulb. He was so silly, he thought to himself, to let his imagination get so carried away. He pulled the string and the thick darkness quickly enveloped him. He took a step toward the stairway when this time he was sure that he heard feet scurrying behind him. He felt a cold chill run down his spine. As he placed his foot on the first step, it creaked. That is when he heard the voice say: 'Don't tell your mother I'm down here!'" Mr. McTeal moaned in a low, weepy voice.

There wasn't a sound to be heard except the chirping of crickets, the croaking of frogs, and the occasional crackle of the fire. As if on cue, an owl hooted in the woods.

"Leroy whimpered, but he bravely took another step. That same voice cried out again to him, warning, 'Don't tell your mother I'm down here!' Leroy answered in a frightened, teeny tiny voice, 'I promise. I promise I won't tell anyone.' Leroy took another step and was just about to dash up the stairway when he felt a cold hand on his shoulder. He slowly turned and he saw…" Mr. McTeal had a serious look on his face and the boys leaned in as he paused for a moment.

"He saw…**BOO!**" he shouted at the top of his lungs.

All four boys reeled backward, as if a bomb had exploded in the middle of the fire. Poodlehead actually did a backward somersault. This was followed by hysterical laughter by all of them.

"You should have seen your face, Poodles! You looked like you got hit with a bazooka!" shouted Benny as he rolled in the grass.

Tucker was proud of his dad. He had gotten them all pretty good. The fire began to die down and Mr. McTeal said it was about time for him to leave anyway.

"Mr. McTeal, why don't you stay out here with us? We have plenty of food!" Benny offered.

Part of Tucker thought that was a great idea. But another part was kind of hoping that his dad would head back home.

"Ha! No, I don't think I'd be able to walk tomorrow if I did that. Besides, I have to go to work tomorrow. I hate to do this, but it's time to put the fire out."

Benny reluctantly grabbed his shovel and started to toss dirt on the flames. The others got sticks and began to stir. Soon, all that was left was a smoldering pile of dirt. Poodlehead went into his tent and got out a battery-powered lantern to replace the firelight.

"Here you go," Mr. McTeal said to Tucker, handing him a cell phone. "You can use it if you have any problems and need to call home."

It was the first time his parents had let him use his cell phone since the sleepover. "Be good," he said, looking at Tucker and then the rest of them. They knew what he meant. He turned and began walking toward home.

An hour later, they were all stretched out on the sleeping bags staring at the stars. They began talking and the conversation took many different turns. It went from aliens to God to the Minnesota Twins to who was the toughest kid in school. Then Benny said something shocking and astonishing.

"So…who do you think is the cutest girl in the school?"

Tucker felt his heart immediately race. He wasn't about to admit what he really thought. That could only spell certain doom or embarrassment down the line somewhere. He'd learned his lesson after Maddy just about spilled his secret. He'd have to think of a good substitute name. Lacey Kapp? No, pretty but too tall and gangly. Aside from that, she had a kind of goofy personality and laughed like a hyena. Ashley Bellizeare? Nice and kind of cute, but a bit on the chubby side. Savannha Foreman? Not bad. She was kind of quiet and…

"I'd have to say Monique Dubois," Josh said. "You're next Tucker. Who do you think is the cutest girl?"

Monique Dubois! Tucker felt a sudden mixture of anger, confusion, and fear. How could this be? Monique could only exist as the cutest girl in the school in his world and no one else's! He was rocked by Josh's admission.

"Uh…uh…" Tucker was speechless. Having to come up with another name and then finding out that Josh had the same thoughts about Monique was just too much.

"C'mon McTeal, pick someone," Poodlehead urged.

"Uh…pass. I haven't decided yet."

"You can't pass; pick someone," said Josh.

"Okay," Poodlehead said, "I'll take a turn. I'll say Kathy Moua."

"What! You can't like her! She's Hmong!" Benny joked.

"Hey, this isn't about who we *like.* You asked who we thought was the *cutest!*" Poodlehead argued.

This was good, Tucker thought. Let them fight about the difference and then they'll forget about me.

"Okay then, I dare you to tell me who you *do* like!" Benny challenged. This was Tucker's chance to change the subject.

"That's not a dare. A real dare is something like daring someone to put their tongue on a frozen pole, or climbing up to the cross bars of the water tower or swimming across the swamp when it has all that green stuff on top of the water. A real dare would be to run through Cowern Woods in the dark."

It was silent for a moment as the others thought about Tucker's suggestions. His plan had worked. No one was thinking about girls anymore.

While no one would outwardly admit it, deep down no one wanted to run through the woods in the dark. It was just too creepy. Who knew what lurked in those deep dark woods after midnight? Even Tucker's imagination got caught up in that suggestion. Maybe there were were-wolves. Or vampires. Maybe even an actual psycho. If you went in there at this time of night, maybe you'd never come back out.

"Okay then, here's a real dare," Poodlehead said with a wicked little smile on his face. "I dare anyone here to run down to the park right now and play around on every piece of equipment at the playground . . ."

"Easy!" Tucker said.

"Big whoop," answered Josh.

"No problem," said Benny.

". . . in your underwear!"

13
NONE BUT THE BRAVE

"WHAT! NO WAY man!" shouted Benny as he laughed. "You're crazy!"

The others howled at the thought of Poodlehead's suggestion.

"Okay, it's on. I'll do it," Josh said, giggling.

"You know I'm in," added Poodlehead.

Tucker had thought Poodlehead was joking, but now that the others had agreed, he felt like he didn't have much choice. After all, what could a quick trip to the park in his underwear hurt? It wasn't any different from a bathing suit, was it?

"I'm in, too," he said.

That only left Benny.

"No way. You guys go. I'll stay here."

"C'mon, Benny. Don't be a buttmuncher!" shouted Poodlehead.

"Dare to run in your underwear! Dare to run in your underwear!" Poodlehead began to chant and soon the others chimed in.

There was no way they were going to let it go. Back and forth it went with the three chanting, only stopping to say that they weren't going without him, and for that very reason he just had to go. Benny would answer back that he just didn't feel like doing it and that he wasn't going to do it no matter what they said or how long they chanted, "Dare to run in your underwear!"

On and on it went until Benny finally got frustrated enough to shout out angrily, "I can't go because I'm wearing Tommy's Barney the Dinosaur underwear!" It suddenly grew quiet.

"Why would you wanna wear Tommy's underwear?" asked Poodlehead.

Benny explained the circumstances.

"All right. If you gotta know, here goes. I took a shower after getting home from fishing and when I checked my dresser drawer I was out of clean underpants. So then I checked my brother Tommy's dresser."

"Dude! Tommy's in kindergarten!" said Poodlehead.

"Duh! Don't you think I know that?" Benny answered defensively. "Well, the only thing left in Tommy's drawers was a pair of Barney underwear. I was in a hurry, so I yanked them up and managed to squeeze into them. I was thinking, 'Who will ever know?'" He paused and looked at their faces. "Yeah, right, who will ever know! So I admit that not only am I wearing Barney underwear, but Barney underwear that are about a hundred sizes too small for me! Are you all happy now?"

Actually, the boys were pretty understanding about the situation. There'd been days when they'd also faced empty underwear drawers themselves. Poodlehead even admitted that there were times he ended up not wearing any underwear at all when he had empty underpants drawers. This made Benny feel better. But just to be on the safe side, he demanded that they take an oath to never reveal the Barney underwear secret.

"You have to swear it. Swear it out loud."

"C'mon, Benny, we're not going to tell anyone."

"I'm not going if you don't swear. You have to swear to something and then spit into the fire."

"The fire's out, Benny," Tucker reminded him.

"It don't matter, you can spit in the ashes. I'm not kidding. I don't want someone like Crandal knowing this—it would be all over town. You have to swear to something."

"Like what?"

Benny thought for a moment.

"You have to swear… you have to swear… that if you ever tell anyone about the Barney underwear that you'll lick the floor around the boy's toilet at school…right after Mr. Heap uses it."

All the boys let out a groan. Mr. Heap was the unusually large, sweaty and hairy gym teacher.

"That's just plain evil!" Poodlehead shouted.

"Man, I feel sick just thinking about that," Tucker said.

The boys agreed, took the oath, and spit in the ashes. Benny took a stick and mixed it all together. A thin whisper of smoke came out of the pile to make it official.

Tucker was thankful now that Crandal hadn't come camping with them. Benny was right. Not only wouldn't have Crandal kept the oath, but he would have come up with some horribly embarrassing nickname for him.

"C'mon, men, time's a-wastin'!" cried Poodlehead as he dashed toward the park in his tighty whities. Josh and Tucker followed in their boxers, with Benny wearing the underwear that could never be spoken of again. They each had a flashlight in their hands that helped them see where they were stepping. They also wore tennis shoes so they wouldn't step on anything sharp in the dark. It was quite a sight.

The dare was that they had to play on each piece of equipment before going back to camp. Tucker chose the crooked slide first, Benny the swings, Josh the merry-go-round and Poodlehead the monkey bars.

"Look at me boys! I'm Captain Underpants!" Benny shouted as he turned his flashlight on himself. He'd evidently lost any embarrassment he'd felt, because he was lying stomach-first on a swing with his arms and legs extended. He swung back and forth as if he was flying. Poodlehead started laughing so hard he dropped from the monkey bars. When he pulled himself together he had to start all over again. The boys were having the time of their lives.

Poodlehead was hanging from the monkey bars again when he was the first one to notice the car coming silently down the road with its lights off.

"Cops!"

"As if!" Tucker said with a laugh. At that very same moment a blinding spotlight hit them all and lit up the playground.

"What in the world…" mumbled the officer as his eyes took in the scene from his vehicle. His mouth hung open. He hadn't expected to see young boys on a playground frolicking around in their underpants in the middle of the night.

"And to think that I thought I'd seen everything," said Sergeant Veid to his partner. Veid was the same officer who came upon Benny and Poodlehead when they were dangling from the snowman's arm in the Kooky Kastle.

Josh sat like a statue on the merry-go-round as it slowly went around in circles. Tucker ducked down behind one of the curved walls of the crooked slide. Poodlehead dropped from the monkey bars and shielded his eyes from the bright light while his tighty whities glowed a brilliant white. Benny hung limply and sadly from his stomach on the swing as it gently swung back and forth, his arms and legs hanging like wet noodles. The officers got out of their squad car and made their way over to the boys.

"What's going on here?" Sergeant Veid asked, unsmiling, with his hands on his hips. The boys just stared back at him, not having any idea of what to say. Tucker laid flat against the floor of the slide and listened. Maybe he would somehow get through this one undetected.

"Okay, guys, come on over here and let's hear the story," Officer Edgar Young said, motioning them to come over. Young was a tall black man with a clean-shaven head and just a hint of grey showing in his neatly-trimmed goatee. "And you hiding on the slide—that means you, too." Tucker allowed his body to slowly slide its way around to the bottom of the slide. Three of the boys walked over to the two officers while Benny continued to stare at the ground and hang limply from the swing as it moved back and forth like a pendulum.

"You over there on the swing in the Barney underpants, get over here," Sergeant Veid ordered.

"I can't," Benny said quietly, without looking up.

"Why can't you?" asked Sergeant Veid.

"I'm too embarrassed."

"You're going to be more embarrassed if we have to carry you over here by your arms and legs. I guarantee you that," Officer Young warned.

Benny slowly put his swinging feet on the ground, stood up and with his head down, made his way over to the other boys and the two stone-faced policemen. There the four stood. Shoulder to shoulder, wearing underwear and tennis shoes. Benny whimpered and the other three looked like they were close to tears.

"Stay right here, boys," Officer Young growled. "Sergeant Veid and I need to confer for a moment." Young quickly turned his back and hurried back to the squad with Sergeant Veid behind him. The officers disappeared behind the bright light that shone from the squad car.

Tucker's imagination ran wild. Were they calling on their radios to set up a cell for them at the jail? Would they be delivered back to their homes in their underwear? The movie began to play in his head. He saw a picture of all four of them on the front page of the local paper. In handcuffs. In their underwear. He saw a police video surveillance tape of them walking into a police station without clothes on. Somehow the video makes its way to the internet for all the world to see. Then he saw himself sitting alone in a jail cell in his underpants. His parents never came to pick him up because they were too disgusted and embarrassed to admit that he was their son.

Tucker wondered how he always managed to get in messes like this. Why couldn't he have just admitted that he thought Monique Dubois was the cutest girl in the school? Then none of this would have happened. It sure would have been easier than going through this.

Tucker focused his attention on the squad car. Twice, the two officers made their way toward the boys. But both times they turned quickly around and went back to the car. The first time it happened, Tucker was hoping against hope that they had received an emergency dispatch call and they would have to leave. The second time it happened, he thought he saw Sergeant Veid begin to laugh before he quickly turned around and walked back toward the car.

Finally, both officers made their way back to the boys a third time. Sergeant Veid looked at Benny and then he looked at Poodlehead.

"Wait a second. I know you two…you two were the ones that took a ride in that inflatable castle and then got caught by the snowman. It's Xiong and Nova, isn't it?"

They nodded.

"I remember that!" said Officer Young. "That was a once-in-a-lifetime catch! I told my wife if that snowman hadn't been standing there at that exact spot, who knows what would have happened to those kids!"

"Nova, your picture was in the paper," Sergeant Veid said. "I see you got that tooth fixed." Poodlehead gave a small smile. Then Veid looked at Tucker and Josh. "And you were their two buddies who followed them on your bikes."

"Yes, sir," Tucker and Josh said together.

"Okay, boys," Sergeant Veid asked as he stroked his impressive mustache, "what brings you guys out here in the middle of the night prancing around in the park in your undies?"

They explained about camping out in the field and the underwear challenge. While it seemed daring at the time, they admitted that right now it seemed pretty stupid.

"So what do you think, Sergeant?" Officer Young asked Veid in a very serious voice.

"I think if I were them, I'd crawl into my tent and call it a night."

"You mean you're not calling our parents?" Benny asked.

"Not unless you want us to."

"No way," Tucker said. "We'll head to our tents right now. We promise, no more trouble!" Deep inside, all the boys gave a huge sigh of relief.

"Hey, Xiong," called out Veid. "You may want to start buying a larger size of underwear. The ones you're wearing can't be too good for your circulation."

"Yes, sir!" Benny called out, and took off running with the others.

14
HIDDEN TREASURES

THE BOYS HAD had a close call and they were thankful that the two officers had let them off so lightly. They knew their parents would not have taken another overnight incident well and might have put an end to them for good.

As the summer days wore on, the crows not only matured physically but also in intelligence and in their interactions with the world that surrounded them. One of Egg's favorite people-games was a game of tag that he liked to play with bike riders. The game would start out with him perching in the old oak tree in the McTeal's front yard or on the roof of their house. The McTeals lived on a corner lot and both perches gave the crow a perfect view of the two streets that intersected there. Egg would then wait patiently for someone to come down one of the streets on a bicycle. He never played this game with strangers, only with individuals he considered to be his friends. As the unsuspecting rider made their way down the street, Egg would wait until they had just biked their way past him. As soon as their back was to him, he would take off from his perch and dive-bomb down toward his unsuspecting target. At the last possible moment, he would pull up and graze the top of the head of his innocent victim. Usually

131

the person would let out a shout or shriek of surprise and look around to see what had happened. Egg would by then be perched atop the corner street sign, clearly enjoying the dramatic reactions from his victim.

Unfortunately, a few of the bike riders would be so surprised by the unexpected tap on the head that it caused them to take a spill off of their bikes. There were no serious injuries, but some of the riders clearly weren't enjoying Egg's game as much as he was. Tucker finally made a couple of signs that he placed out on each side of the yard that read: "Beware of Diving Crow!" This helped remind anyone biking down the road of Egg's peculiar game, so that riders were no longer caught off-guard. Once the bikers stopped being so surprised, they no longer reacted so dramatically when he would skim the top of their heads. This evidently took the fun out of the game for Egg and he decided to move on to other things.

One of those other things was Mr. McTeal. Ethan McTeal liked to tinker. It could be just about anything. It might be a car, a lawnmower, a hairdryer, or a child's toy. He also liked working on these things outside if possible because the sun provided a strong light in which to view smaller objects.

Egg, like many other crows, had a deep love and fascination with shiny objects and he quickly discovered that Mr. McTeal was a good source of these little treasures when he was outside fiddling with something. The picnic table was his preferred place to work on objects and that suited Egg just fine since one of his favorite perching spots was on the rain gutter just above that very table.

There Egg literally had a bird's eye view of every little shiny widget or thingamajig that Mr. McTeal had laid out on the table. He would watch and wait, and when Mr. Mc-Teal would go in the house for a drink of water or for any other reason, Egg would fly to the table and choose the most appealing treasure for himself. Before Mr. McTeal would make it back out the door again, Egg would take the gleaming prize in his mouth and be long gone.

"I think I'm losing my mind," Mr. McTeal shouted one day. "I know I had a bolt on the table. I know I did!"

"Maybe you grabbed it when you came in," Mrs. Mc-Teal said. "Have you checked your pockets? Have you looked in the grass under the table?"

"Yes! And I've retraced my steps and looked in every spot where I may have set it down."

"Well, maybe little gremlins are stealing them," she said sarcastically. Little did she know she wasn't that far off.

"Is Poodles there?" Tucker asked. He'd phoned Poodlehead and figured maybe they'd head up to the junior high and play some tennis. Tucker was pretty bored and Poodlehead was the only one of his friends who could actually hit the tennis ball back over the net on a regular basis. Poodlehead came to the phone and agreed to meet Tucker at the school.

"Should we bring Robin and Egg?" Poodlehead asked.

"Sure, why not? They're probably as bored as we are."

"Okay. I'll bring my racket and meet you up there."

The junior high was only a couple of blocks away, so Tucker hustled and pulled out his racket and a can of tennis balls from under his bed. He decided it would be easier to walk than to ride a bike and try to carry everything. Aside from that, Egg would be riding on his shoulder and if the bike got going very fast, Egg would just hop off and fly away. It didn't seem to take much for Egg to fly off these days. Tucker had even started to see him interacting with the wild crows that would land in the oak tree in the front yard. They'd caw and Egg would caw back and occasionally follow them somewhere.

Tucker walked the two blocks and crossed Holloway Avenue and met Poodlehead at the corner. Egg and Robin cawed a greeting to each other. The group then made their way up toward the sidewalk past the west side of the school.

Maplewood Junior High School had an indoor swimming pool and there were always people coming and going because the pool entrance was there. As they neared the building, Tucker could see two figures carrying towels and walking toward them. He could tell it was two girls. As they drew closer, it appeared that the one on the left was Lacey Kapp. Funny, Tucker thought. Her name was one of the names he'd considered using when Benny wanted everyone to confess who they thought was the cutest girl in the school when they were camping out. She still looked just as tall and gangly to him. But maybe she wasn't as goofy anymore.

The other girl was…was…he stopped in his tracks.

It was Monique Dubois!

What was she doing over here? *Going swimming obviously*, he said, answering himself. She and Lacey must have been dropped off. In fact, as he quickly glanced to his right, the driver in the car that just drove past him looked like a high school version of Monique.

"Hey, why are you stopping?" Poodlehead asked.

This was the very moment that he had dreamed about.

"Oh...nothing. Rock in my shoe."

Everything was perfect. Tucker had even remembered to put on some underarm deodorant right before he left. This had to be fate! Egg just happened to be sitting on his shoulder, looking blacker and sleeker than ever! She'd have a million questions about Egg, just like everyone always did, and he'd be more than happy to answer every one of them. Step by step, they drew closer. He put a sly little smile on his face as the girls approached. He was ready for her first question or comment. Monique looked at him, then at Poodlehead, and then at the birds, as did Lacey.

"Hey McTeal, did you know you and your weird albino friend have got stupid-looking blackbirds on your shoulders?" Lacey barked. Then she broke out in her hideous hyena laugh.

Tucker was speechless.

Poodlehead gave Lacey a look of disgust. He popped out his front tooth, opened his mouth wide and let out a loud obnoxious laugh. It was a perfect imitation of Lacey and it was so loud that it startled Robin and Egg and they flew off to a nearby tree.

Lacey blushed red and the big smile fell from her face.

"Jerk."

The two girls turned the corner and were gone.

Tucker felt numb. He had played out this scene many times in his mind, but it had never gone like that. Lacey Kapp was an idiot times ten. She not only messed up his opportunity of a lifetime with Monique Dubois, but she didn't even know the difference between a blackbird and a crow. And why did she call Poodlehead an albino? Tucker wasn't even sure what that was. He started to take a step to leave when he was shocked to see Monique poke her head around the corner.

She whispered to him, "Don't pay any attention to her; she's kinda strange sometimes," and then disappeared again.

His legs and knees felt a little shaky. Why did Monique say that? Did she just feel sorry for him? He wasn't sure if he should feel happy or sad about what just happened. Her words did help make him feel a bit better, regardless.

"Did you see the look on Kapp's face when I gave her that laugh? I thought the missing tooth was a nice touch, didn't you?"

"Uh…yeah. Nice." Tucker was lost in his thoughts and barely heard what Poodlehead was saying.

"Hey Tuck, what's an albino?"

"I don't know, Poodles."

They continued on their way toward the tennis courts. Tucker tried to play a few games of tennis, but his heart wasn't in it. He complained to Poodlehead that he was tired and then made his way back home.

* * *

A few days later, Tucker was lying on the couch in the living room reading some old comic books when he heard his dad shouting about something as he came in the back door.

"I knew it! I knew it! I wasn't crazy! It was that bird! He's the one who's been stealing my stuff!"

Uh oh, thought Tucker. This doesn't sound good.

When Tucker came into the kitchen, he was actually surprised to see a smile on his dad's face.

"I'd been trying to fix that back door latch because the door wasn't catching when it closed. I finally took the latch out and was taking it apart on the table. I started to go in the house to get a needle-nose pliers from the basement and then remembered I had one in the garage. Well, as I'm coming back out the door, I see Egg on the table with my small Phillips screwdriver in his mouth! He sees me and then takes off over those trees!" he said, pointing toward a neighbor's backyard.

"Dad, you sound almost happy about it," Maddy said.

"In a way, yes, I am. I was starting to think I was going a bit nuts because I kept losing parts and pieces when I was working on things and now I know it wasn't me!"

Tucker looked out where his dad had pointed. He had an idea. He grabbed a can of dog food and went out the door.

"Where are you going? Can I come?" asked Maddy.

"You know, that actually might be a good idea."

"Yeah!" Maddy shouted.

As they walked through neighbors' yards, Tucker told Maddy about what he was thinking.

"In my reading about crows, I learned that they are kind of like pirates. They like anything bright and shiny and when they find it, they hide it like buried treasure."

"Cool! You think Egg has buried treasure?"

"Well, he probably doesn't bury it, but I'm thinking he may be hiding his treasures somewhere." They kept walking until they were in a spot where they could see fairly well in all directions.

"Egg hasn't eaten since this morning, so I'm thinking he's hungry." Tucker smiled and looked at Maddy. "We may be able to get an idea of where he is stashing his plunder," he said with a pirate accent. Tucker again looked around in all directions. "Okay Maddy, hold up the can and call for Egg."

She did as her brother said. They waited for a moment, but no Egg.

"You know what, Maddy? I think Egg is pretty careful about his treasure. I'll bet he's hungry, but he's also worried that we're going to see where he is coming from. I have an idea of where he might be, so let's turn around the other way and face our house." They both turned and faced the opposite direction.

"Now call him. If I'm right, he'll come flying up right behind us."

Maddy held the can up again and called for Egg. Sure enough, seconds later he came flying over their heads and landed on the ground in front of them.

"Boy, he's smart. The books were right," he muttered.

"What are you talking about?" Maddy asked.

"I'll tell you later. What I need you to do now is to put Egg on your shoulder and start feeding him as you walk toward home. I don't want him to see where I'm going and get angry with me if I find his secret stash." Maddy did as he said and made her way toward home. Tucker began walking in the direction that Egg had come from.

Years ago, he and a friend had built a tree house near here. The friend had moved away a couple of years back, but the tree house was still there. He wondered if Egg had found that place and then decided that it would be a good place to hide his loot.

When Tucker got to the tree house, he began climbing up the wooden stakes that were still left in the tree. Many were missing and the ones that were left were rotten and crumbly from their years of being exposed to the sun, rain and cold. He had to be careful as he climbed. He made it to the tree house door and belly crawled through it to get inside. It felt good to be back in his old place. He ran his fingers over the plywood wall. "I'd almost forgotten about you." It was smaller than he remembered. He took a deep breath in through his nose. Yes, it still had that musty wood smell to it. It brought him back to the proud day that he and his old friend Randy had put the last nail in the tree house and how they had talked as if they would live there forever.

He looked around the little room and there was no treasure to be found, just some comic books with missing covers that appeared to be missing half of their pages. Oh well, it was a good hunch and it had been nice seeing his old tree house again and reliving a few memories.

He was belly crawling out backward with his legs dangling out the door when he had another idea. He crawled back in and stood up in the doorway. He pulled himself up and then on to the top of the tree house's flat roof. There, in the back corner, he saw what looked like a piece of an old shingle. He lifted up the shingle and underneath it was what looked like an old discarded nest.

"Why, Egg, you sneaky old pirate," he said out loud.

In the nest were all of Egg's precious treasures that he had been collecting and then hiding. There was a broken clam shell, a gumball ring, two bobby pins, three screws, one bolt, numerous metal washers, one penny, two dimes, a small wire spring, a piece of broken green glass, a small polished agate, a house key, a shiny piece of aluminum foil, and at the very top, a small Phillips screwdriver. He took the screwdriver, but placed everything back exactly as it had been and then put the shingle back on top of the nest.

He looked in the direction of his home and said, "Your secret is safe with me, my friend," and began to climb down off the roof.

15
A Murder of Crows

IT HAD PASSED the midpoint of August and summer was already giving hints that it would not stay forever. Even though the days were muggy and warm, when the sun went down there was a soft coolness in the air on some evenings that had not been there just a few weeks before. Radio ads began to advertise the upcoming Minnesota State Fair, a sure sign that summer was drawing to a close. On this particular Saturday afternoon, the boys found themselves headed for the basketball court in Northwood Park.

"Two on two or PIG?" Benny asked.

"I vote for PIG," Tucker said. "It's too hot to be running up and down the court." Josh and Poodlehead agreed. Egg, Moe, Midnight and Robin rode on each of the boy's shoulders. As they entered the court, Egg flew off Tucker's shoulder and landed right on the rim of the netless hoop on the south side of the court and Moe followed. The boys could have gone down to the other side of the court, but the hoop that Egg and Moe were sitting on was their favorite for playing PIG because the backboard was more forgiving with bad shots. Midnight and Robin flew over and landed in the grass that grew between the court and the old warming house and began pecking at the ground, apparently looking for worms or bugs.

"Snap! I never thought of that," Poodlehead said, referring to Egg's and Moe's decision to sit on the hoop. "Maybe we should have left them at home."

"Nah, this shouldn't be a problem," Josh said as he grabbed the basketball and lobbed it gently at the backboard. As soon as the ball made contact with the metal, the loud bang and the vibration sent the two startled birds flapping away into a nearby oak tree. Egg cawed out a few loud complaints to show his displeasure at being treated so rudely. Moe saw Egg's example and decided to join in with the cawing.

"Aw, they'll get over it," Poodlehead laughed. "Josh, you go first since you got them out of our way."

Egg and Moe eventually got over their anger and decided to join Midnight and Robin in the grass. The game of PIG was a close one, but in the end Josh made a highly improbable no-look-over-his-head-backward-shot from the foul line that could not be duplicated. The shot gave Tucker and Benny their final letter and Josh the win. Poodlehead had a cold shooting hand and had been eliminated quickly.

"Okay boys, let's get serious," Poodlehead announced. "Next game is HORSE, so Josh can't get lucky with his junk shots."

"Junk shots? A basket is a basket. You're just mad because you got spanked that last game," Josh answered. "But it doesn't matter to me. I'll smoke you all in HORSE as easily as I smoked you all in PIG!" he said with a grin.

"As if!" Tucker shouted with a laugh. "Bring it!"

Poodlehead's ever present smile left his face. He dribbled out to the foul line and let go a jump shot. The ball swished through the hoop and would have caught nothing but net—if there had been a net. Josh followed and sunk his shot. Tucker's shot hit the front of the rim and bounced back. Benny took a shot from the three-point range and put it in. The game of HORSE had begun and there was an intensity that had been missing in the previous game. Each boy took careful aim, not wanting to be the first one eliminated. Poodlehead, despite his fast start and boasting throughout the game, was again the first one gone. Tucker was next. That left only Benny and Josh, and both of them had the letters HORS. The next one to sink a shot that was not duplicated would win the game.

Benny started from mid court, dribbled a bit and then took a jump shot from the foul line. The ball hit the backboard, bounced off it and then through the hoop.

"You are dead meat!" Tucker shouted to Josh. Benny retrieved the ball and tossed it to Josh.

"As if!" Josh said as he caught the ball and gave a quick smile in Tucker's direction. Josh dribbled from mid court and, like Benny, took a jump shot from the foul line. The ball sailed cleanly through the hoop.

"You lose!" shouted Benny. "You didn't hit the backboard!"

"You never called backboard!" Josh said. They went back and forth until Poodlehead and Tucker intervened and agreed that Benny indeed should have called that shots needed to be exactly duplicated. So the game went on.

The crows were finding plenty to do. Egg had landed on top of the white boards that surrounded the hockey rink and Moe soon followed. Inside the rink, they spotted a rabbit lazily chewing on the grass on the other end of the rink and they decided to take turns swooping down at it from behind and touching its back. The startled rabbit would jump straight up in the air. Much like the bike riders Egg loved to annoy, the two crows enjoyed watching the reaction of the rabbit. Robin and Midnight continued to find things of interest in the grass between the court and the warming house. Moe had swooped down on the rabbit and had just landed on the south end of the rink when a glowing reflection in the grass from a candy wrapper caught his eye. It was next to the warming house in the grass and not far from Midnight and Robin.

"Say goodnight, Benny!" Josh shouted as he sailed a one-handed shot from mid court. It slammed against the backboard and then hit the rim with force. The ball shot five feet straight up in the air before coming down, bounced back and forth on the rim a couple of times and then fell in.

"No!" Benny hollered as he grabbed both sides of his head.

"Oh, yes!" Josh answered.

"As if!" Tucker shouted.

"You and your junk shots!" said Poodlehead.

"Okay Benny, let's see you match that!" said Josh.

Moe saw that Midnight and Robin were not far from the shiny piece of foil that he had spotted in the grass and flew over toward it, wanting to grab the precious crow treasure before they did. But as he flew over to the spot, the sun no longer reflected on it at the same angle and the gleam from it disappeared. He landed and began to search for it closer to the warming house.

Benny stood at mid court. The air had become hot and humid and sweat was dripping from his face. He stared intensely at the rim, measuring in his mind the distance he would have to throw the ball. Too hard and it could go over the backboard. Too soft and it might not even make it to the hoop. He bounced the ball a few times, trying to convince himself that he could do it. Josh looked on with a confident smile on his face, believing that the game was his. Tucker and Poodlehead sat in the grass silently rooting for Benny because Josh seemed to win these kinds of games too often.

Moe's eyes carefully searched the grass as he made his way toward the corner of the building. The sun again caught the edge of the aluminum wrapper and it shimmered briefly in the light. He hurried toward the treasure before any of the other crows could take it for themselves.

Benny placed the ball in his right hand and cocked it behind his head. He again measured the distance with his eyes. A couple of deep breaths and then the ball would be on its way.

* * *

On the south side of the warming house sat a large metal storage tank. Years ago, the tank was filled with oil and it was used to heat the railroad car in the winter so that the children skating at the rink would have a place to warm their frozen toes and fingers. A gas furnace long ago replaced the need for the tank, but the old tank remained on the side of the building. It rested on old railroad ties that formed a kind of hollow box. The railroad ties were not attached to the building, so there was a small gap between the ties and the building. This gap was just wide enough for a certain animal to squeeze in and out of and to make the box one of his homes. For quite some time, its two angry eyes had been watching the four boys playing basketball and the four crows looking for food. That animal was a large and very nasty cat that many people called Evil Caesar.

No one can be sure why he did what he did on that day. Evil Caesar was one who was seldom seen; he very rarely came out when humans were around. Maybe it was because he remembered that these were the same four boys who robbed him of his four meals earlier that summer. Or perhaps it was just that he saw that the opportunity was there and that it was so close that he could not resist it.

Moe hurried toward his gleaming treasure and snatched it in his beak. In a blinding second, a grey flash came shooting out from under the tank. Moe, who had been so focused on his shiny jewel, never saw what hit him.

Benny looked at the hoop, took one more deep breath and started forward.

"Aaw, aaw, aaw, aaw!" came the hysterical screams of Egg, Robin, and Midnight. The boys had been around them enough to know that these were very panicked calls and they all turned to see what the problems was. To anyone else, all the crows looked the same. But the boys knew each crow by their different features. Egg was larger than the others. Robin's beak was a bit longer. Midnight's feathers were a bit darker in color. Benny, with the ball cocked behind his head, had just taken a first step toward his mid court shot when he heard the screams and looked that way. He froze at the sound of the frightened calls of the birds and saw Evil Caesar rolling on the ground with black feathers in the air and he knew. The big cat had Moe.

"Tsis ua!" Benny screamed. "No!"

Benny ran toward Evil Caesar and Moe with the basketball in his hand. When he was about twenty feet away, he threw the ball at Evil Caesar as hard as he could. It was a direct hit and the stunned cat was sent tumbling off the bird. Benny saw a piece of an old broken hockey stick on the ground near the warming house and grabbed it.

Evil Caesar rolled quickly to his feet, hissed and howled and showed his teeth. His eyes looked like they were on fire. He arched his back and puffed out his fur, which made him look even larger than he was. He started back toward his victim. Benny stood defiantly over Moe as he shouted angrily at the cat in Hmong. Egg, Robin, and Midnight were now diving at Caesar and cawing. Evil

147

Caesar was not about to lose his dinner this time and he charged back in an attempt to snatch Moe. Benny swung his stick at him, but missed. Evil Caesar's sharp claws caught Benny's pants and tore them as he made his pass and avoided the stick. Evil Caesar howled and wailed. No one had dared ever challenge him like this before.

It had all happened in a matter of seconds and Tucker, Josh, and Poodlehead were looking for anything they could find to drive the cat away. Tucker found a branch with leaves on it and ran over to Benny. Poodlehead grabbed an old tennis ball and Josh, who couldn't find anything, finally just took off one of his shoes. Poodlehead threw the tennis ball and hit the cat in the side, but Evil Caesar never even flinched. Josh threw his shoe, but it missed its mark and sailed over the cat's head. His other shoe went wide. Evil Caesar now circled them as they protected Moe. He was looking for an opening to grab the bird and run off with him. All the boys were shouting at the crazed cat and Tucker took a step toward him and shook his branch. The crows were diving down at him, too.

Finally, all the noise and commotion distracted Evil Caesar enough so that even through his blinding rage he realized he could not win this battle today. He began to back up, hissing and growling and baring his ugly yellow fangs. He dashed around to the other side of the warming house and then across the dead-end road into the tall grasses of the field. Egg, Robin, and Midnight chased and dive bombed him until he disappeared into one of his many hiding places.

Tucker looked over at Poodlehead and Josh. A smile crept on his face.

"We did it!" Poodlehead shouted. "We defeated Evil Caesar and saved Moe!"

They all turned to look over at Benny who had been standing over Moe to protect him. Benny got down on his knees to see how Moe was doing. He could tell right away that something was wrong. Moe lay still and his neck was turned in an unusual way. Benny knew at once that he was dead. He stroked Moe's head and began to cry. He then laid face down in the grass, crying into the crook of his right arm with his left hand on top of Moe. Egg, Robin, and Midnight returned and landed near Moe's body. They cawed and clucked and nudged Moe to encourage him to get up. Tucker, Josh and Poodlehead stood near, watching quietly.

After a while, Tucker asked Benny if he was okay. Benny wouldn't look up; he just shook his head no and continued to cry into his arm while he stroked Moe's head.

"I think you better get his dad or mom," Tucker said quietly to Poodlehead. Poodlehead nodded and took off toward Benny's house. If he cut through yards, Poodlehead could make it to Benny's house in under five minutes.

Soon Poodlehead returned, saying that Mr. Xiong was on his way.

"I saw Maddy playing in the O'Connell's yard and told her what happened. I figured since she helped raise Moe, too, she should know."

It wasn't long before Benny's dad came walking across the baseball field toward them. He was wearing green work pants and a white t-shirt. He had a worried look on his face as he neared the boys and then spotted Benny lying on the ground. He bent down and placed his hand on Benny's back and spoke something softly to him in Hmong. Tucker could see Benny shake his head no. Tucker wondered if he had asked him if he was hurt. Mr. Xiong rubbed his hand over Benny's back for a while and again spoke quietly to him in the Hmong language.

Finally he said, "Come, Kong. You are brave boy," in English.

Benny raised his head from his arm. His eyes were swollen from crying and his face was red. He and his dad slowly got to their feet. Egg, Robin, and Midnight nudged Moe a couple more times and then seemed to understand that he was dead. They cawed and then Egg flew out in the direction of Cowern Woods with Robin and Midnight following right behind him.

"Why are they leaving?" Benny asked.

"They go tell friends," Mr. Xiong said.

A squad car could be seen coming down the dead-end road. A neighbor who lived near the park had heard the commotion and looked out her window to see the boys fighting off the large cat and had called the police. As fate would have it, Sergeant Veid and Officer Young responded to the call. They saw Benny and his dad standing near Moe's body and asked what had happened. They had heard a couple of months ago about how the boys had rescued the four crows from Evil Caesar and they were saddened to find out that the big cat had now killed one of the birds. Officer Veid's eyes narrowed and he stroked his thick white mustache.

"Something's got to be done with that cat. He's been terrorizing this town for too many years and I'm just plain tired of it," he said.

"I know he's just trying to survive, but he's becoming bolder as time goes by," Officer Young added. "Just last spring he got a hold of a mother duck and her ducklings near the swamp by the nursing home. That nasty cat just about scared one of the old folks to death when they came out to try to stop him. He hissed and growled and acted like he wanted to eat them, too."

"Look," Tucker said, pointing toward the woods, "they're coming back!" As Egg, Robin, and Midnight came back from the woods, Tucker could see about seven or eight more crows following right behind them. They landed in a tree above Moe.

"Are these some of your friends?" Sergeant Veid asked with a smile.

"Well, three of them," said Josh.

"Look, here comes some more," said Poodlehead as he pointed to about ten more crows making their way toward them from the woods. They too landed in the trees.

"There's about ten more," Officer Young said, pointing to a group coming in from the direction of the baseball field, "and five more coming up over by those houses! What's going on here?"

Mr. Xiong looked around as more and more of the crows began to appear from all directions. He patted Benny on the shoulder.

"I told you. They go tell friends."

"But why are they all coming here?" Benny asked.

"Crow funeral," said his dad with tears in his eyes but a little smile on his face.

Soon the trees in the park were filled with crows. It wasn't long before they covered the roof of the warming house and were lining the boards of the hockey rink. They now seemed to be coming from everywhere and there were hundreds of them.

"I've never seen anything like this," said Tucker.

"That because you never looking," Mr. Xiong said.

Maddy arrived at the park and slowly walked over to Benny and his dad. Her eyes were red and her face was wet from crying. She slowly turned in almost a full circle as she took in the sight, but she didn't say a word. Then she looked down and saw Moe crumpled on the ground and then looked up at Benny.

"I'm sorry about Moe. He…he was a good crow and a good friend." Then she began to sob. Tucker went over and put his arm around her.

The voices of the crows grew louder and louder as their numbers multiplied. Later, people from a mile away claimed that they could hear the sound. At the point where it seemed to grow to be the loudest, Egg, Robin, and Midnight flew out from the tree that they'd been perched in. At the very instant that their feet hit the ground, everything grew silent. Not one caw from one crow could be heard. All of the crows' eyes were trained on the three as they walked toward Moe's broken body. Egg stopped in front of him and then Robin and Midnight stood on each side.

Egg lifted his wings and cawed loudly. As soon as the last cry came from Egg, the multitude of birds that had filled the trees left their perches and the sky was suddenly black with crows. Yet ten seconds later, there wasn't a crow to be seen except for Egg, Robin, and Midnight.

Sergeant Veid looked at Officer Young and said, "If I hadn't seen what I just saw with my own eyes, I'd have never believed it." Officer Young nodded in agreement and they made their way back to their patrol car.

16
THE BEST SUMMER EVER

BENNY'S DAD HAD his arm around him and he had a warm and gentle look upon his face. Tucker had never seen Mr. Xiong look this way before. Then he heard him talk to Benny.

"Kong, sometime I have been hard on you. Life is hard and I wanted you to be ready. I wanted you to be strong. But I think I forget things. I forget what it like to play and have friend. I forget what it like to be young."

Tucker was surprised again. He had never heard Mr. Xiong say that many words in his life.

"I see how you care for your bird and how he care for you. When I was small boy in my village, I watch crow every day and I know how smart he is. Hmong people all know that crow very smart. We tell old story of how crow trick tiger and other animals. When I small boy, I think to myself," he said as he tapped his head, "maybe crow be my friend, too. So I try to catch him," he said, slightly smiling for the second time that day, "but he always too smart for me and it never happen. But seeing what happen today help me remember. Help me remember when I was young and happy and life not seem so hard. I think it time for me to change." Mr. Xiong bent down, picked

154

Moe up gently and said, "Come Kong, we will bury Moe in backyard and make sign for grave." Mr. Xiong began walking back toward home. Benny's eyes met Tucker's. He then gave a small nod to Maddy and the three boys and followed his dad home.

Tucker heard a knock on the back door as he worked a crossword puzzle in the living room. He heard his mom answer the door and then the voices of what sounded like adults.

"Tucker, door for you!" he heard his mom call.

As he entered the kitchen, he could see Sergeant Veid and Officer Young standing on the back step.

"Hey, buddy, we have something we thought you might like to see," Sergeant Veid said.

Tucker had no idea what it could be. He followed them to their car and they opened up the back door of the squad car. There was a blanket covering what appeared to be a large rectangular box sitting on their back seat. Officer Young pulled the blanket off and there in the cage sat the legendary Evil Caesar.

Tucker was startled and took a step backward.

"Snap! How'd you get him in there?"

"That part was actually pretty easy. We got the Parks and Recreation director to place live traps in the areas we thought the nasty old cat might be living. We baited it with cat food and it didn't take too long," said Officer Young.

"Well, we did also catch a few other neighborhood cats, a raccoon, and a dog before we hit the jackpot," said Sergeant Veid.

"I'm kind of surprised," Tucker said as he leaned in closer to the cage. "Why isn't he growling and hissing and going crazy?" Evil Caesar just sat in the cage and stared calmly back at them.

Both policemen laughed.

"Oh, believe you me, he was!" Officer Young said. "He was like a caged demon. You should have seen him! He chewed on the wires, he howled and spit, he hissed and banged himself back and forth against the cage. You'd have thought he was the Tasmanian Devil himself!"

"Yeah, he was so out of control that we thought he was going to seriously injure himself. So we stopped by the vet clinic and old Doc Nelson gave him a shot of something that made him as mellow as a baby lamb!" Sergeant Veid explained. "You still might not want to pet him though," he joked.

"So...now what is going to happen to him?"

"We could have dropped him off with Doc and he could have put him down, but somehow that didn't seem right," Sergeant Veid explained. "It isn't his fault that he is the way he is. But a wild animal with the personality of Evil Caesar doesn't belong in a town like North St. Paul. I have a buddy that is heading up north tonight and he offered to drop him off in the woods near his cabin. There are plenty of mice and rabbits to keep him well fed up there and he won't cause any problems because he won't be near any people."

"Well," said Officer Young, "we were passing by this way and thought you'd like to know. You and your friends can rest easy now when it comes to your crows. Make sure you let them know."

"Sure," Tucker said, "and thanks for stopping by."

They threw the blanket back over the cage and shut the door. They hopped in the car, backed out of the driveway, and drove off. Tucker was about to go back in the house when he saw Egg come streaking over some trees and land on the gutter. He was glad Egg hadn't been here a few minutes ago; he might have caught another glimpse of Evil Caesar and that was something he shouldn't ever have to see again.

"Caw, caw!" he called as he stared at Tucker. Tucker knew by that tone and the look on Egg's face that he was hungry.

"Okay, I know what you want," he said, walking to the door. "Let me find a can of dog food and I'll be out before you know it."

"As if!"

Tucker turned and looked around the yard. He was sure he had heard someone say something. Seeing no one, he went in and opened a fresh can of food for Egg and went back out. He was feeding Egg when he saw Benny coming up the street and he was carrying what looked like a blanket in his arms.

"I can't believe it! I can't believe it! Look what my dad got me!" he shouted with a big smile on his face as he began to run toward Tucker. When he reached Tucker, he opened the blanket. It was a little white puppy.

"He's a pug just like Bandit! My dad knew I've always wanted a dog! I still can't believe it!"

"Wow, Benny, that is totally awesome!" Tucker called for Maddy and his parents who quickly came out to take a look, followed by Olivia and Emily.

"He looks just like a little Bandit," Maddy proclaimed. "What's his name?"

"Well, I named my crow Moe, so I thought I'd name him Curly. He's my favorite Stooge, plus he has a cute little curly tail."

"He's the cutest puppy ever," Maddy said.

"As if!"

"What do you mean?" Benny asked Tucker.

"I didn't say that," he said.

"Yes, you did, I just heard you."

"As if!"

This time Benny could see that the voice hadn't come from Tucker. It had come from the direction of the gutter that was just above them.

"Did Egg just say, 'As if'?" Benny asked.

"No…how could he…?" Tucker began to answer before he was interrupted by Maddy.

"Yes, he did! I found out that crows can learn to talk like parrots; it was in one of the books you brought home, Tuck. This is just the first time he's said it in front of anyone but me. I've been practicing with him ever since we got him. He's even started to say other things that I never even taught him! I thought it'd be funny for him to say "As if" since Tucker says it all the time."

"I do not!"

"Yes, you do!" everyone said.

"As if!" he answered back with a little smile on his face.

"What other things does he say?" asked Mr. McTeal.

"You'll find out," Maddy said with a sly smile on her face.

They all admired Curly for a while longer until Benny said he wanted to show Curly to Josh and Poodlehead, too.

"Wait, before you go Bandit should meet his new friend!" Maddy said. She ran into the house and carried Bandit out. He did much the same thing as he did when he first saw the crows. He did a lot of sniffing and then began to lick Curly.

"Okay, that's enough Maddy. The boys want to go," said Mrs. McTeal. "Bandit hasn't had a potty break for a while; as long as he's out here why don't you just hook him up to the chain before you go in."

Maddy attached Bandit's collar to the chain. The boys went on their way and Mr. and Mrs. McTeal, Maddy, and the girls went back inside.

Bandit did his business and then he heard a voice say, "Here, Bandit!" Bandit hurried toward the backyard. He looked around and didn't see anyone, so he wandered toward the side of the house again and lay down.

"Here, Bandit!"

Bandit got up and trotted over to the backyard again. He looked around and seeing no one went back to the side of the house.

This routine repeated itself a few more times until Maddy stepped out the back door and said, "Egg, you stop calling for Bandit or I won't teach you any more new words!"

Benny and Tucker first made their way to Josh's house and then they went to Poodlehead's. Josh came with them. They were all a bit surprised when who should come walking up Poodlehead's driveway but Crandal Bino-Grimes.

"Dudes, what's happening!" he shouted. "Long time no see. Where you guys been hiding?" It was an odd thing to say, since Crandal was the one who had pretty much disappeared for the last three months. But they learned long ago that Crandal lived in his own world that had its own strange rules.

"So you got a mutt, eh, Benny? Good luck with that!" he said, hardly taking more than a quick glance at Curly.

"I bet you guys can hardly wait!"

The four boys looked at each other and had no idea what Crandal was talking about.

"Wait for what?" Tucker asked.

"Gimme a break, quit pulling my chain! Today is the day! You are free! The games are back on!"

It stunned the four boys that they could have forgotten the ban on their video games was over.

"My mom bought *Hit Men From Hades* just for the occasion and I broke it in last night. You are not going to believe what is in this game! First off…"

Tucker could see Crandal's lips moving, but he wasn't really listening as Crandal went into detail after detail about the game. He couldn't help but notice how red Crandal's lips were. It was because there was such a contrast between his lips and his pale, pasty face. He looked over at Poodlehead, Josh, and Benny and saw how the sun had painted their faces different shades of brown. Even Poodlehead, who normally had rather pale skin, had color in his face. Benny was thinner now than when the summer began. Tucker also noticed how pudgy Crandal had become. He used to be about the same weight as Josh.

Crandal continued to go on and on about all the characters in *Hit Men From Hades* and all the adventures they were all going to have again when they started playing tomorrow.

"Dudes, it is on! We are going to *live* again!"

The phrase brought Tucker back to the start of summer. It had seemed like the end of the world after the sleepover and then having to take care of the crows. He thought about their encounters with Evil Caesar, chasing Benny and Poodlehead as they flew off in the Kooky Kastle, camping out in the field and even getting caught running around in the middle of the night in their underwear. He wouldn't trade what happened over this summer for anything.

But his best experience of all was finding and raising Egg and the other crows. If he had played video games with Crandal all summer, none of the things he experienced would have ever happened. It wasn't that he now disliked video games. In fact, since Crandal brought it up, he was looking forward to finally finishing that long-delayed game of *Revenge of the Rabid Leprechauns*. It was just that this summer made him realize he didn't want to build his life around any game.

"Maybe later, Crandal. I have to give Curly a bath," Benny said.

"Josh and I started building a maze for the crows to go through yesterday," Poodlehead said. "They'll have to ring bells and pull strings to open doors and get food. We thought once they learned how to go through it, we'd video it and put it on the internet. Why don't you help us?"

Crandal was stunned beyond words. He figured that his friends had been counting down the days to get back to playing video games with him. He couldn't understand their lack of interest.

"A crow maze? You gotta be kidding me! Poodles! Josh! Did you hear me? I just bought *Hit Men From Hades!* Tuck, at least I know you are in."

"Sorry, Crandal, I'd really like to, but I promised my mom I'd cut the grass when I got back home. I'll give you a call later." Tucker was glad to see that Crandal had decided to start coming around again.

"See ya, guys. You got a nice dog, Benny."

"See ya later, Tuck," Poodlehead, Benny, and Josh said. Crandal didn't say anything. Tucker started back toward home.

"Hey, Tuck, wait up," Crandal said, jogging a bit to catch up. The boys walked for a ways, saying nothing.

Finally Crandal said, "So, what's the deal? What'd I do to get you guys to chump me like this?"

"Chump you? What are you talking about?"

"You know what I'm talking about. You guys go three months without playing video games and then pretend like you didn't even know today was the day you get to play them again. Yeah, right! You're planning on getting together today and playing without me, aren't you?"

"What? Playing games without you? We never…"

"OK, Tuck, I'll admit it if that's what you want. I was mad at you. I was ticked at all of you. But how was I supposed to feel when you show up at my door with your very own crows? What was I supposed to do, go to the crow store and get one for myself? Maybe it was partly my fault for not showing up the morning you guys found the crows, but there wasn't anything I could do about it afterward. I knew I wasn't in the "crow club" and that I was always going to be odd man out with you guys after that."

Crandal's explanation and sudden openness caught Tucker completely by surprise. He had no idea that Crandal had felt that way. It explained a lot, especially his behavior the day they had stopped over at his house to show him the crows.

"Crandal, you got it all wrong. We're not planning on doing anything without you. But you have to understand, a lot of things have changed over the last three months. We haven't played any games since early summer, so we aren't even thinking about them right now. We didn't

163

mean to exclude you this summer. Honest. Remember, I'd call you and you're the one who never wanted to come."

Crandal didn't say anything for a while as he thought about what Tucker had said. Finally he asked, "Do you mind if I come over and see your crow?"

"Sure, Crandal. Egg always enjoys visitors."

When Tucker got home, he went in the house and pulled two hotdogs out of the refrigerator. He went back outside and broke one of them up and handed the pieces to Crandal.

"There is nothing Egg likes better than hotdogs. Even if he's not that hungry, he can't resist them." Tucker held his hotdog over his head and called for Egg. There was a flash of black in the sky and within seconds Egg was on Tucker's shoulder cawing loudly, eying his favorite treat. Maddy heard the noise and went outside.

"Go ahead Crandal, give him a piece of hotdog," Tucker said.

"What do I do? Do I toss it in the air?"

"No, just put it near his mouth and he'll take it," Maddy said.

"He won't bite me, will he?" Crandal asked nervously. Tucker laughed and remembered how nervous he was the first time he fed Egg.

"Go ahead Crandal, you're perfectly safe."

Crandal cautiously moved his hand toward Egg. Egg eyed the piece of hotdog and quickly snatched it out of Crandal's fingers. He flipped back his head and gobbled it down while making a loud "Gawba, gawba" noise. He looked at Crandal and began cawing loudly.

"Does that mean he wants another one?" Crandal asked.

"Another *one?* Try another ten! He loves hotdogs," Tucker said. Crandal fed Egg another, this time less cautiously.

"Dude! This is so awesome!" Crandal continued to feed Egg the rest of his hotdog and then asked Tucker for the other piece. Tucker not only gave him the hotdog, but moved Egg to Crandal's shoulder. About this time, Poodlehead walked into the yard. He came at an angle where he could see Tucker, but not Crandal and Maddy.

"Hey Tuck, I'm out of dog food and I was wondering if I could ...hey!" Poodlehead could hardly believe what he was seeing.

"Crandal, you look like a pro already!"

Crandal smiled and fed Egg his last piece of hotdog. Egg sat on his shoulder and cawed, hoping for more. When he realized Crandal's hands were empty, he stopped his noisy begging and made some grumbling little crow noises.

"Buttmuncher!" he shouted and flew off.

Poodlehead's mouth dropped open.

"Excell-aun-tay, grome-ay-graun-tay!"

"See, I told you he learned other words," Maddy proclaimed.

Tucker just stood there with a huge smile on his face. It really was the best summer of his life.

Made in the USA
Charleston, SC
29 June 2011